■ □ ■ □ ■

THE SOUL OF A PATRIOT

■ □ ■ □ ■

EVGENY POPOV

THE SOUL OF
A PATRIOT

OR

VARIOUS EPISTLES

TO FERFICHKIN

Translated from the Russian by Robert Porter

NORTHWESTERN UNIVERSITY PRESS

EVANSTON, ILLINOIS

Northwestern University Press
Evanston, Illinois 60208-4210

First published in Moscow by *Volga* No. 2 1989 under the title *Dusha patriota ili razlichnye poslania Ferfichkinu.* Copyright © 1989, 1994 by Evgeny Popov. English translation first published 1994 in Great Britain by Harvill, an imprint of HarperCollins Publishers Ltd., copyright © 1994 by HarperCollins*Publishers.* Northwestern University Press edition published 1994 by arrangement with HarperCollins Publishers Ltd. All rights reserved.

Printed in the United States of America

ISBN 0-8101-1203-5 CLOTH
ISBN 0-8101-1193-4 PAPER

Library of Congress Cataloging-in-Publication Data

Popov, Evgeniĭ.
    [Dusha patriota, ili, Razlichnye poslaniia Ferfichkinu. English]
    The soul of a patriot, or, Various epistles to Ferfichkin / Evgeny Popov ; translated from the Russian by Robert Porter.
        p. cm. — (Writings from an unbound Europe)
    ISBN 0-8101-1203-5 (cloth : alk. paper). — ISBN 0-8101-1193-4 (pbk.)
    I. Porter, Robert. II. Title. III. Title: Soul of a patriot.
    IV. Title: Various epistles to Ferfichkin. V. Series.
PG3485.2.P557D8713   1994
891.73'44—dc20   94-18887
                                                          CIP

The paper used in this publication meets the minimum requirements of the American National Standard for Information Sciences—Permanence of Paper for Printed Library Materials, ANSI Z39.48-1984.

TRANSLATOR'S INTRODUCTION

It is rare for a short novel to capture completely the spirit of an epoch. It is rarer still for the comedy in a work which focuses on one brief moment in history to be enhanced with the passage of time. Yet it would not be extravagant to make both these claims for *The Soul of a Patriot*. The blend of family chronicle, autobiography, political-philosophical commentary and actuality gives Evgeny Popov's work both intensity and universality. On the surface, the narrator, one Evgeny Anatolyevich Popov, is simply dashing off letters ("epistles") to an old acquaintance, recalling family anecdotes from pre-Revolutionary Russia, recreating scenes from his childhood and youth, or relating current events as they unfold. However, behind the jaunty, offhand style, fluctuating at will between the lyrical, the awkward and the bawdy, there is the sure hand of a master craftsman, the writer Evgeny Anatolyevich Popov.

The death of Leonid Brezhnev on 10 November 1982, was the event that inspired him to write his novel, and the world is still gauging the historical impact of the Soviet leader's demise. Brezhnev's two immediate and short-lived successors, Yury Andropov and Konstantin Chernenko, provided a suitably lacklustre coda to his eighteen-year conservative rule, before Mikhail Gorbachev assumed power in 1985 and ushered in an era of "openness" and "restructuring". *Glasnost* and *perestroika* became part of the international vocabulary.

The Soul of a Patriot is about many things, but at its heart it is concerned with the death throes of the "era of stagnation" – Gorbachev's euphemism for the attenuated neo-Stalinism that pertained under Brezhnev. One product of the utterly transformed cultural climate was the publication of this novel in 1989. Many people in Russia – and elsewhere no doubt – sensed the import of Brezhnev's death, but few could have even guessed at the substance of its precipitious aftermath, and perhaps only

Evgeny Popov has to date been able to record in artistic form something of the spirit of Brezhnevism and the first shock waves that were felt at its demise. Gogol's famous satirical play *The Government Inspector* caught the essence of the petty tyranny, corruption, provincialism and plain absurdity that dominated Russian life under Nicholas I, the most repressive of the nineteenth-century tsars. *The Soul of a Patriot* performs a similar service to history. Moreover, in some ways the work has proved to be eerily prophetic.

Yet it would be a mistake to take these "various epistles to Ferfichkin" too solemnly. The Soviet critic Sergei Chuprinin, in his afterword to the first publication of the novel, wrote that "in Evgeny Popov absolutely everything is subjected to trial by laughter or to testing by intentional duping", and he found the novel remarkable first and foremost by virtue of its freedom ... "freedom from any regulation and any inhibitions. Its freedom which is unobtrusively opposed to any red tape or dead-headedness or any looking over your shoulder at what its reception might be or what people might think about it." Perhaps the real hero of Popov's novel is the same as the hero of Gogol's play: laughter.

Those who know something about Russian literature will start off confidently enough. There is a character called Ferfichkin in Dostoevsky's *Notes from Underground*. But our narrator states that he knows little about the addressee of the epistles, while insisting that he is important, whereas the narrator himself is not. We are told precious little about Ferfichkin, and it becomes clear that he has nothing to do with Dostoevsky's character. The "informed" reader is the first victim of Popov's jokes and false trails. Yet the narrator is sure that Ferfichkin is a stickler for factual accuracy, and hence we are treated intermittently to lengthy catalogues, complicated arithmetical calculations and attempts at clinically precise description ... only to be told from time to time by our informant that he knows nothing, can't remember and keeps getting mixed up.

On one level we are dealing with a delightful parody of conformist Soviet writing, which, according to the theory of Socialist Realism, must be factually correct, complete and objective, but which in practice often amounted to whitewashing. In the first epistle, the narrator's excruciatingly full list of all the Caucasian peoples can be taken as a swipe at Stalin's own leaden style, while the suggestion that all these national minorities are "friendly" betrays a hideous irony that has become all the more poignant in the last four or five years. Yet, on another level, we are also dealing with an Evgeny Popov – standing behind the narrator Evgeny Popov, a different person altogether, so we are told – whose business is with much more than straightforward satire. In interviews Popov has listed among his favourite writers Laurence Sterne and Mikhail Zoshchenko.

Sterne's resolute refusal to formulate a conventional plot, the typographical eccentricities of *Tristram Shandy*, the melancholy wanderings of the author's childhood, his occasional debauchery and even his practical piety as a clergyman find more than an echo in *The Soul of a Patriot*. Popov the late twentieth-century novelist is not alone in seeking some inspiration in the eighteenth century.

Like Popov, Zoshchenko may be described as a satirist, yet in each case the term is inadequate. In his stories of the 1920s Zoshchenko charted with nothing short of genius the gap between ideals and actualities in Soviet life. Grappling with the newly formulated jargon that the authorities peddled, Zoshchenko's common man sought more often than not to justify and rationalize his own age-old egocentricity. Beneath the slogans and pomposity there was in fact little regard for the collective or for the public weal. Since the late 1980s there has been widespread recognition in the Soviet media that the great social experiment, which clearly Zoshchenko among many other writers had grave misgivings about from the start, has gone catastrophically wrong. Here Popov comes into his own. His tightly packed narratives show us a Russia where little has changed in the human psyche despite all the social engineering. Pretending that all is well, ignoring the lessons of history and attempting to repress uninhibited dialogue on social issues have merely exacerbated social and psychological ills.

No wonder then that in *The Soul of a Patriot* a good many characters are confused or absurd, and that their identities are in doubt. Often, with disquieting, Kafka-like discretion, they are designated only by an initial. Some of them are real enough, notably D.A.Prigov, but others are composites, while others, perhaps unduly well known in the narrator's view, are given corrupted forms of their names. No wonder, too, that in Popov's prose there is a studied contrast between the sophisticated, carefully wrought, grammatical structures and the banal, bawdy subject matter they encapsulate. Or that phrases in block capitals, so reminiscent of the political slogan, stand cheek by jowl with the language of the gutter. The result is a highly refined bathos. Brezhnev's funeral – a religious ceremony in all but name – is described for us merely in note form, as if the hypocrisy of it is unworthy of the author's true literary skills.

However, the narrator's voice is not always irreverent, and at times one detects an unmistakeable note of sincerity and humanism. Asked in a recent interview how he viewed the "new" literature, Popov replied that it was "calmer, less angry, less social" and he hoped that literature would at last become "neither Soviet nor anti-Soviet" but would "fulfil its true destiny, which has been lost in the 'heat of battle': to serve as a mediator between God and the earth which mortal man treads."

The Soul of a Patriot contains numerous thumbnail biographies of the narrator's ancestors and acquaintances, and not a little autobiography. But we should bear in mind the narrator's self-confessed shortcomings, and that he distinguishes between himself and the writer of the epistles. Given this kind of double bluff, a brief note on the real Evgeny Popov and the context in which he has operated over the years is all the more appropriate, and will make many references in his novel a good deal clearer.

Evgeny Popov was born in 1946 in the Siberian city of Krasnoyarsk which spans the river Enisei. From 1963 to 1968 he studied geology in Moscow. He tried but failed to enter both the Gorky Institute of Literature and the Institute of Cinematography. From 1968 to 1975 he worked as a geologist in the vicinity of his home town, and then moved back to Moscow. Though he had published sporadically in local newspapers and journals since the early 1960s, his real literary début came in 1976 with the publication of two of his short stories in the leading literary monthly *Novy mir*. The stories were introduced by the hugely popular Siberian writer and actor Vasily Shukshin. However, Popov's period of Brezhnevite respectablility was short-lived. In 1979 came the *Metropol* affair. More than twenty authors contributed to the almanach of this name (which was edited by Vasily Aksyonov, Andrei Bitov, Viktor Erofeev, Fazil Iskander and

Evgeny Popov) and requested that it be published without the usual cumbersome procedures involving bureaucracy and censorship. When permission was refused, the work went promptly into samizdat, and was also published in the West. Punishments of varying severity were meted out – Popov and Viktor Erofeev were expelled from the Writers' Union, which they had been permitted to join only months previously. Aksyonov emigrated to the West.

Though collections of his short stories were published abroad, as far as the Soviet reader was concerned Popov was now a nonperson. But as *The Soul of a Patriot* demonstrates, he was far from idle. With the advent of Gorbachev and *glasnost* Popov became, along with a great many colleagues, freer than he had ever been before to publish the work that had accumulated in his desk drawer over the years.

Popov is not of the younger generation of writers – they hardly emerged under Gorbachev, not least because the journals were too busy publishing the backlog that had built up during the years of repression. Yet he is one of the leading representatives of the "lost" generation, those writers who should have made their mark during the period of stagnation, but, as Ferfichkin's correspondent, with characteristic awkwardness, would put it, "because of circumstances which were nobody's fault" failed to. The point about the Brezhnev era, as far as literature is concerned, was that there were inconsistencies. There was indeed general repression – Sinyavsky and Daniel imprisoned, Solzhenitsyn forcibly expelled from the country, many others banned and harassed into emigration. Yet other writers – good writers – were able to continue to operate, and even flourish. Some had been the firebrands of the literary thaw following Stalin's death (poets like Evgeny Evtushenko and Andrei Voznesensky). Others, such as the best of the "village prose" writers or Yury Trifonov, published work of outstanding quality and told unpalatable truths. All this must have been doubly frustrating for Popov and his kind. Honest, talented people were being quietly smothered – they had no international reputation, acquired in the more liberal days of Khrushchev, to protect them, and they had no pronounced Russian nationalism, as exhibited by the village prose writers, which might endear them to their cynical political masters. Thus their qualities were on display only in private conversations, in informal gatherings, over a drink or two ... Here was a genuine sub-culture, with none of the pejorative overtones that that term acquired in the eighties in our own society.

The Soul of a Patriot captures the atmosphere of Brezhnev's Russia, but it also goes some way to setting Brezhnevism in a broader context. Popov's seemingly endless excursions into his family's history raise familiar questions of Russia's place in Europe and her own sad past. Boorish nationalism and general ignorance mingle with sensitivity and genius. We may or may not be prepared to believe that Uncle Kolya astonished the city of Vienna by cooking the most mundane of Russian dishes, but we are not allowed to forget that Russia produced Mandelstam and Tsvetaeva.

Finally, – and perhaps overriding all these vexed and abstruse issues that Russian writers so often concern themselves with – *The Soul of a Patriot* manifests, behind all its jokes and parodies, the simple human quality of congeniality. The lengthy toast with which the novel closes contains only one significant omission – Stalin. The narrator might well take the view that without a measured degree of brotherly love all the scope for human development generated after Brezhnev's death could well be lost.

ROBERT PORTER

Bristol
31 December 1993

THE SOUL OF A PATRIOT

LET ME START sort of right at the beginning. Well, let's suppose there's this man. He sort of writes artistic works. That is, like he sort of used to write and he even had acquaintances and contacts in the literary world, so he's extremely proud of this and he's always name-dropping. But nowadays he sort of like doesn't write due to circumstances which are nobody's fault, but just composes epistles to Ferfichkin.

It's not important who this person is. He could just as well be Pseukov, Fetisov, Garigozov, Kankrin, Shenopin, Galibutaev, Rebevtsev, Kodzoev, Telelyasov, Popov, or even somebody else. It doesn't matter. He insists his first names are Evgeny Anatolyevich. That's my name as well, but that doesn't matter either. There can't be any doubt among those who know me that I'm not him, and likewise any other personages mentioned by him don't correspond to any real living people, but are just the fruits of his idle imagination and his occasional tall stories. It's not important.

What is important is the addressee of the epistles – Ferfichkin. Who he is, one can't say – and where he lives, what his job is, and also how old he is, no one knows. Unfortunately, the author hasn't considered it necessary to divulge the identity of the addressee, which at times creates the impression that he doesn't know it himself.

There's no point in explaining how I got hold of this one-sided correspondence. In the first place I've given my word not to, and in the second place nobody would believe me anyway. Just let me say that the author of these epistles has

3

given me his permission to do whatever I like with them, and I would just like to note in self-justification that I emphatically dissociate myself from some of his escapades and skylarks, if they are going to cause anybody any unpleasantness or irritation, for these days, of course, a lot of the things that he writes to Ferfichkin about have changed completely. A new indefatigable life has illuminated our steep banks, and part of our sorrow has, now and forever more, vanished into the oblivious sea of the distant, or perhaps the recent, past.

So then! ...

EVGENY POPOV

Moscow
31 December 1983

25 October 1982

. . . so then, dear Ferfichkin! You won't understand this, but I'm still in luck. Some of the windows in the other carriages on the train have been completely knocked out. And also, about seven years ago, you see, there's been some brawling in here: there are still faint traces of blood on the doors half off their hinges, though it's not impossible that it's the paint work from previous years, it could be anything, I emphasize this, knowing that you value the accuracy of my descriptions.

The river, which I took hypothetically to be the Don as in Sholokhov, really has turned out to be the Don (quiet, it REALLY has turned out to be quiet, for example, as quiet as the river Kacha, which in my homeland, the criminal district of the Siberian town of K., flows past the meat-processing plant and through the Tartar quarter). Autumn is stifling everything, it's as if there's been no summer at all: we passed Rostov, the dull Azov Sea glittered. Feast your eyes on this, Ferfichkin, there it is, Taganrog-1 railway station. The Russians here wear fur hats and the cold makes the denim-clad Caucasian youths hop about. I'VE REMEM-BERED: someone said to me a little while ago in Moscow; "If I'm not mistaken, your name's Zhenya, isn't it?" – "No,"

I replied, "You're wrong, my dear friend! I used to be called Zhenya about ten or twenty years ago, when there was everything before me, but I've changed my name and now I'm Evgeny Anatolyevich, these days I've got a bald patch that covers half my head and a crooked beard . . ." He didn't understand, took offence and gave me a SIGNIFICANT look. I wonder, did he REALLY take offence, what do you think, Ferfichkin, or was that faint grimace of his merely the result of the transience of life that we've already mentioned? I'd like to have your opinion because I myself don't know . . . I don't know . . . I don't know . . . I only know that now we are approaching Ilovaiskaya station, because we've already gone through Amvrosievka, and it was night when we reached Krasnodar. Yesterday at eight o'clock in the evening we left Tuapse, at ten o'clock we went through Phanagoreia which was dark ("Fine people the Phanagoreians!" as Emperor Somebody the Something said, I can't remember which one. Maybe you remember which one it was?) And now it's the Don. The Quiet Don. Along the bank of the Don roamed a young cossack . . . Stenka Razin, 1671, executed . . . Alexei Maximovich Kaledin, 1918, shot himself . . . A prosperous locality but patently tight-fisted people. At the stations the cossacks sell lovely big melons for three roubles each . . . You shouldn't do that, comrade toiling cossacks, for "we're all brothers, but our father, you see, has gone to sea" (S. Anderson). There, travelling along your road, are Moscovites, and other Russian gits, as the Ukrainians would say, including in particular my good self, Evgeny Anatolyevich, a native of the town of K. which stands on the great Siberian river E. which flows into the Arctic ocean, but we've got less money than you, so you have to put yourselves in our position. After all, even the friendly Caucasian peoples: the Abkhazians, Adzharis, Adyghians, Armenians, Balkars, Greeks, Georgians, Imeretians, Ingushians, Kabardinians,

6

Karachays, Koreans, Lakks, Tats, Persians, Svanians, and Chinese all offer lower prices than you do, and you're our brothers by blood and by religion. It's wrong, wrong, wrong . . .

Well, anyway, it can't be helped, Ferfichkin! Chalk slopes. The autumn forests are a painting shading into a drawing. A straw-coloured, yellow oak leaf, mangled and blowing along the ground. The weeping willow is green. Southern plants are green, northern ones are yellow. Now and then, don't you wonder how the other regions of the State are getting on at any given second? Central Asia, the Urals, Siberia, the Far East, where the island of Shikotan is, which a colleague by the name of Gorich used to tell me about, the fish called a "chavycha" and a plant called "ipritka" which gives you an intermittent fever and makes your temperature fluctuate wildly? . . .

Well, anyway, it can't be helped. Don't lose your temper, Ferfichkin, but I'm still going to go on nattering about everything that comes into my head, since I've got nothing else to do now. However, for your edification, I'll spell it out: I'm travelling on the Tuapse-Moscow express and I'm thinking about the money-box which I recently acquired in the covered market in Voronezh for my niece Manya. I spend manee for Manya . . . Hee-hee-hee . . . Give me an assessment of that awful pun, my friend . . . Assess it and forgive me my nervous, hesitant laughter, Ferfichkin . . .

Listen, the money-box herewith is in the shape of a plaster-cast girl, a shepherdess. It's about twenty-five centimetres high, the girl is sitting, with her ample skirts spread out and she's clasping her little round knees in her brownish little arms. Her little scarlet lips are slightly opened, her little white teeth are shining like pearls, there's a devil-may-care look in her eye. She's wearing a cap decorated with

7

little flowers, and each little plaster-cast flower has its own immanent colour, yet the whole thing cost only five roubles, for I drove a hard bargain with that drunken Voronezh peasant. A generous hand will slip coins into the great big slit at the side, and when the time comes for our little Manya to get married, the money-box will be broken open with a deft blow, and a tidy sum, built up over the years, will be revealed, that is of course unless they bring in another currency reform like they did in whatever year it was – 1947? or 1961? ... Or was it 1947 and 1961? ...

I'm on my way, travelling, travelling ... I send words of greeting to you from this dirty railway carriage, my dear friend! ... "I've left you, my dear ones ..." An erudite, clever man like you, Ferfichkin, will have guessed of course, where this quotation comes from, and it will be no secret to you that all the foregoing is an elaborate time-honoured prologue to my epistles to you, and that I myself am ACTUALLY on my way back from a business trip to the Caucasus, which I capped off with a 235% overfulfilment of the production plan ...

... and where, in the time that I had free from the most strenuous of work, I swam in the sea, gnawed exotic nuts, and partook of southern fruits and vegetables. I'm paying for all this now, being shaken about as I am in this smashed up railway carriage: the wind is coming in through the windows, the doors, the ceiling and the floor. And I'm travelling north, gentlemen! ... O evil sorrow, why hast thou overcome a man away on business! The mere thought of meeting my ardently beloved wife warms my frozen soul! Outside the window, foreign parts race by, and the Ukrainians standing there make V signs at us (signalling of course V for victory) as they watch the train speeding away. Tsoi, the Korean manager of the sovkhoz, has concluded an agreement with me, but has neglected to sign it, which fact has only come to light now I am on my way back, so now I'm going to get it in the neck from the boss, but do you remember, Ferfichkin, that this is a situation that has already been well worked over in literature? ... On the platform at the end of the carriage a drunken citizen is praising two young men, much given to laughter, for the fact that they are Georgians, a friendly, wealthy people, who lead clean lives. But he asks them not to offend the Russians. They promise not to. I'm not being ironic, Ferfichkin, this is a really clear, convincing example, a good, instructive lesson for young people! Some tasteful countryside: Tuapse Bay looks wondrously beautiful against the background of the sun receding into Turkey, especially if you have a drink of "Anapa" wine on the pier – 1 rouble 80 kopecks a bottle (0.75 litre), 19° proof. Lovely fortified wine, I hear you smirk. Pity you weren't with us, you'll hear me smirk. We would make a lot of new friends in this town – there are sailors, railway workers, shop assistants, policemen. We'd have to work very hard. We'd eat *khachapuri* cheese pie, and wash it down with "Anapa". "It's silly to regret what we've never had," you'll reply, and I won't argue with that.

Let me just say that *Letters of a Russian Traveller* by Mr N.Karamzin makes clever, useful reading for anyone who wishes to broaden his perceptual horizons with the aim of preserving an aura of culture! ... Efficacious reading ... The sun is setting. The sun is setting, the steppe is bathed in light, the citizen on the platform at the end of the carriage is shouting that he is a Russian, the seed of the Zaporozhye wide open spaces, the son of Taras Bulba. Which one? Ostap? Andry? And now we're in Voronezh, its streets are straight and full of elegant buildings. Mandelstam lived here, and Mandelstam lived there, and there's no Mandelstam here, and there's no Mandelstam anywhere, so

9

Natalya Evgenyevna Sh., a beautiful sixty-year-old woman, tells me. She's intending to cook green cabbage soup, we go to the famous covered market in Voronezh, where they roll the barrels into the cellar down a sloping cement floor, and where in the gloomy halls they sell everything under the sun, at skyhigh prices ... Radishes, fennel, parsley, onions, cabbages ... A little way off looms the drunken Voronezh peasant morosely overseeing his plaster-cast wares: V.Tyorkin, J.Stalin, and the MONEY BOX as described above and acquired as below for Manya. I fall in love with the money box immediately and go over to ask about the price. "Ten!" hazards the peasant in a resolute voice. "Eight," he says, correcting himself. Before I can stride off, he is selling the money box to me for five roubles, and fussing around as he wraps it up, telling me how to hold it so that the fragile object doesn't get broken. "It's kitsch," I explain in embarrassment, but Natalya Evgenyevna doesn't hear me. She is thinking about Osip Mandelstam, who has consecrated her life. Dear, dear Natalya Evgenyevna! ... Oh, Ferfichkin, oh, Osip Emilyevich, oh ... so what, it doesn't matter ...

... But actually I wanted and I still want to talk about something else, and I feel ashamed, Ferfichkin, to think of you wrinkling your brow in annoyance and being forced to read these inaccurate, scrappy lines. I wanted to and I still do. Talk about something else. So right, I'm going to talk about something else. I'll tell you, Ferfichkin, about the money box. Or rather, about TWO MONEY BOXES, one of which came to an end on 5 January 1961, since it was broken open then on the occasion of the currency reform they were bringing in, and the second, which had only just started its life, since I had only just bought it at the covered market in Voronezh. These money boxes were like two peas in a pod, but I can distinguish between them and I love them.

Now that I've at last given you an explanation, my dear friend, and you understand everything completely, I'll continue with my epistles to you, and they perhaps ought to start with Uncle Kolya, who in 1945 utterly astonished the Austrian city of Vienna.

26 October 1982

Well now, somehow I ought to explain to you that this is in no way a "flashback". Or rather, it is a "flashback" of course, but at the same time it isn't. In terms of the subject matter, it's a typical "flashback": 1946, 1950, 1956, 1960, but it's only functional, isn't it? . . . To cut a long story short, I've got mixed up and I'm getting you mixed up too. I'd better say right away: it was in fact

UNCLE KOLYA

who utterly astonished the Austrian city of Vienna with the phenomenon known as:

HOME-BAKED MILK

and brought back from the war that very money box that we'll call for the time being the shepherdess No.1. I was born in January 1946, and in February 1946 Uncle Kolya the billiard player came back from the war, and he brought our family as a present the "war booty" money box, which came my way.

Uncle Kolya was born in 1919 and was Mama's "cousin", if that word is still in use at all anywhere in the territory of the State. A good-looking 1930s lad, he was pretty frequently to be found in the billiard hall in the Gorky Central Park of Culture and Rest. Uncle Kolya was a good player,

11

but he only gained definitive success 10–15 years later, that is, after the war. Uncle Kolya was in the war. After the war he reached his peak, but by the end of the 1950s his glory had faded somewhat. His drinking became a bit heavier and a bit less refined. On top of that, a younger breed came into the billiard hall in the Gorky Central Park of Culture and Rest to oust the veterans. Then Uncle Kolya became a Lovelace. He would tell Aunt Masha that he was going on a business trip, and she would pack a case for him. But then, once during an alleged business trip to the distant town of TAGANROG (!) (Note that I emphasize that name) he was discovered in the Tartar quarter near the meat-processing plant; there Uncle Kolya emerged one morning from a wooden cottage that was submerged in white Siberian snow, wearing felt, soled boots and a sleeveless padded coat, he stepped out sedately, looking innocently at the world around him and, carrying two empty buckets, he headed for the nearest standpipe, which was cold and covered in ice. There it was, unfortunately, that he was discovered by a female friend of Aunt Masha, who promptly informed her of the encounter. Aunt Masha grabbed the washing line and ran into the woodshed. No one was surprised. She didn't even have time to tie the noose round her neck before they pulled her out of it. She was always trying to hang herself week in and week out, but never mind, she's still alive for the time being, God give her strength! ...

Aunt Masha was also in the war. For some reason she always recalled the war with a woman's lightheartedness, she loved singing the lyrical songs of M.I.Blanter, B.A. Mokrousov and V.P.Soloviev-Sedoi, and in moments of particular festive enthusiasm, which quickly degenerated into vulgarity, she always sang some indecent couplets concerning an old woman and a cavalry regiment. She used to call these couplets "the hussar's words". Her mother-in-law – that is, Uncle Kolya's mother, old Mother Tanya, my great aunt once removed – worked in the medical department of the Red Cross and the Red Crescent, she was a sister of mercy in the First World War and knew the polar explorer Papanin. And her husband, old Grandad Vanya, indirectly my great uncle once removed, had also served as a medical orderly. In the second decade of our turbulent century he went out "on cholera duty", chamber pot in hand, the "night-time vase" as this item was decorously referred to in price lists, and his semi-literate village landlady, a Siberian woman, cooked him some tasty Siberian ravioli in this pot, having mistaken the "vase" for one of those new-fangled saucepans they had in towns. Grandad Vanya puked. Uncle Kolya worked at the mechanics factory as "a supply engineer". He and Aunt Masha brought their children up lavishly. They bought them a harmonium for a 1000 old (pre-1961) roubles. I'm not going to describe these children. It's boring ... But there again, why not? The younger daughter Valka was a fat, sleepy girl, she's an engineer now as well, and her husband is an engineer too with some ideas he's proposing for rationalizing industry. And the elder girl, Sonka, born in 1950, shamed her family in 1968 by bringing home an elderly, bald man, a land-surveyor and topographer, and announcing that "this is my husband". Uncle Kolya shoved him down the stairs, and since then Sonka has shut herself off from everything. She finished school with a gold medal, then made use of her harmonium lessons by going to work in a kindergarten as a "music teacher". To start with she was neo-Russian Orthodox, but then she joined a sect of Christian Baptists which was organized by a young art group in the town of K. – painters, stage-performers, rock-climbers. But the sect fell apart because of mutual intolerance and theological disagreements among its members, and how Sonka lives now or what she believes in,

13

I've no idea. She got up my nose at one time in my life, so now I'm getting my revenge on her in these pages, taking advantage of my privileged position as the author of these epistles to you, Ferfichkin. Here's a HYPOTHESIS: my cousin once removed headed a "Zen" group after she broke away from the sect of Christian Baptists, and she became an anti-social element, but it's not impossible that in fact she married my childhood friend Khrulev, stole him from his wife, and the newly-weds went off to work in Mongolia, and came back from there with a nice new Zhiguli car. Well, she's probably old by now, that Sonka, well, she'll be – 1982 minus 1950 equalls 32. No, she's not old . . .

. . . The Austrian city of Vienna! You and I, Ferfichkin, have never yet been to the Austrian city of Vienna, which is why I don't know what the name of that restaurant was where Uncle Kolya astonished the public there that time. Uncle Kolya used to say that it was the "very best restaurant in the Austrian city of Vienna".

THE YEAR 1945. Two Soviet officers went into the very best restaurant in the Austrian city of Vienna. Victorious soldiers, they looked around benevolently and calmly at the noisy crew there: the cut-glass, the silver, the starched serviettes, the low neck-lines and jewellery of the ladies. A gipsy made his way from table to table, pressing his violin to his cheek.

The head waiter in full evening dress, looking like the singer Vertinsky, emerged, as it were, from out of the ground.

"Pleesse, pleesse, my dear seers," he said in broken Russian, sweetly screwing up his eyes with exaggerated pleasure.

The officers seated themselves.

"What offer you I can?" continued the head waiter in the same language.

The officers looked at one another.

"Well what have you got?" asked Uncle Kolya, clearing his throat importantly.

"Oh, vee have everyzink," responded the Austrian. "Succulent hams, French oysters, the finest trout – the fruits of mountain streams, bananas from Hong Kong, figs and pears from Italy, pineapples, champagne, whisky, gin. We have everyzink."

"You can't have," said Uncle Kolya with a frown, and his comrade, a major, moustached, swarthy and handsome, who had spent the entire war disseminating counterpropaganda in German, gently tugged at his sleeve to tip him the wink: these people are on our side, they're not Germans, they're Austrians ...

"You can't have," said Uncle Kolya a second time, perfectly capable of understanding the international situation without any help from the major.

"But vee have can," insisted the head waiter, at this point permitting himself some condescension, for at last he felt he was on safe ground. "Vee have can. And if vee have not, then our chefs will prepare any dish you care to order."

"Any?"

"Any."

"Kebabs?"

"Kara Sea kebabs? Cutlet kebabs? Basturma beef kebabs?"

"What about cabbage soup?"

"Day old? Green? Ural? With nettles? Ukrainian borshch with pancakes, with garlic, with cayenne pepper and a drop of the hard stuff."

"Siberian ravioli?"

"50% beef, 30% mutton, 20% pork, onion, pepper, bay leaf, marrow bone, add seasoning and herbs, vinegar, mustard ..."

"Black radishes?"

"In kvas."

"Pudding?"

"With a dessert sauce."

"Duck?"

"Peking."

"What about HOME-BAKED MILK?"

"Vertinsky" halted and mopped his sweat-covered brow dejectedly. He had lost the competition. Uncle Kolya went out into the kitchen and personally prepared the home-baked milk, and treated all those present to some. And all those present, including the major, were astonished, praised this famous Russian dish, had nothing but admiration for Uncle Kolya and gave him a round of applause. A misty-eyed beauty (diamonds, pearls, a coral rose in her luxuriant hair, a Russian "Kazbek" cigarette in her mouth) invited Uncle Kolya to dance the czardas with her. She was a countess of the ancient noble line of Esterhase. Uncle Kolya sang:

> As if I were a coward,
> As if I were really scared
> Of the lad
> Wearing a crane's feather
> In his
> Hat

DISCREETLY THE WAITERS BUSTLE, FULLY AWARE OF THEIR ESTEEM, VIOLINS REFLECT THE CUT GLASS, WHILE THE CHAMPAGNE AND VODKA GLEAM (N.Fetisov. From the narrative poem "The Gestapo Man and the Wolf", 1972, Manuscript, Krasnoyarsk.)

*

16

"And incidentally, home-baked milk is very easy to make. Simply take some milk, pour it into a dish, pot, or any other earthenware container, and place it in the plate warmer of a traditional Russian stove which has just been allowed to go out, and leave it there for any length of time," explained Uncle Kolya, adding angrily: "And don't interrupt me by saying there isn't a traditional Russian stove to be had in Vienna, and therefore no old-fashioned plate warmer to draw in the residual heat from the stove. I'm telling you, it was the best restaurant in the Austrian city of Vienna, and they really had EVERYTHING there, and the only thing that they didn't have and didn't know about, seeing as they didn't have it and didn't know about it was

HOME-BAKED MILK,

so I taught them, and now they know, and now they really have got absolutely everything . . ."

Oh, Uncle Kolya, Uncle Kolya! Just imagine, Ferfichkin, that he once told me how he caught 85 pike in 2 hours. The success of the lucky fisherman was easy to explain: a spring of mineralized waters flowed into the lake from which he caught 85 pike in 2 hours, and the temperature of the spring in mid-August was $-18°C$.

"How many degrees, Uncle Kolya?"

"Minus eighteen."

"But Uncle Kolya, water freezes at zero, that's what they taught us in school . . ."

"Really? Are you sure?' chuckled Uncle Kolya condescendingly. "And what temperature does salt water freeze at?"

"It isn't eighteen degrees, is it?"

"I don't believe that you don't believe me," said Uncle Kolya, getting worked up. "Look here, you must, you must believe me! We dipped a thermometer in the spring

17

and it showed exactly 18°C. Minus! ... That's the whole secret ..."

What secret? How come? I don't understand. But if "I must, I must", then OK, I believe you, no problem. You've known me for a long time, Ferfichkin: there was a time when I said what I thought, but now I think what I say. I believe. And you must believe that Uncle Kolya astonished the Austrian city of Vienna, that he caught 85 pike in 2 hours, and brought home to our family a present of the painted plaster-cast shepherdess No.1, about 25 centimetres high, sitting down, with her ample skirts spread out, and clasping her little round knees in her brownish little arms. Her scarlet little lips were slightly opened, her little white teeth shone like pearls, there was a devil-may-care look in her eye. You must believe, you must! You have to believe in something after all, Ferfichkin. Do you remember us talking about that once in the kitchen? Oh, Ferfichkin! ...

27 October 1982

GRANDAD PASHA,

who destroyed an animal by the name of

PUSSY CAT MYTH

was a *kulak* who'd survived everything and was a hero of Port Arthur. He always condemned his nephew, my Uncle Kolya, for telling lies, because he himself was considered a wise-cracker and hoaxer. Scraping his feet along in their calf-skin boots he used to come and visit us in winter, and instead of saying hello, would ask us children: "Kids, you don't know whose horses those are out in the yard, do you? There's a troika with bells on it, the horses have got red

18

ribbons tied in their manes, you can see their breath, and there's straw in the sledge? ..."

We would dash outside headlong. There were no horses. Quietly we would come back into the house, where Grandad Pasha, both he and his George medals radiant, would be sucking tea from a glass through a piece of sugar in his mouth and drinking vodka from a small, blue, faceted glass.

He squashed my kitten. This is how it happened. The neighbours' cat Murka had produced a litter behind their stove, and we had a kitten from it, and we called it Myth in honour of the then darling of the public, the famous French singer Yves Montand, about whom there was an exposé recently (1982) in some newspaper, revealing the true face of this alleged former friend. Yet at that time he was very popular, and the famous Mark Bernes, now deceased (1969), even sang a friendly song about him on the radio.

> The pensive voice of Montand
> Is heard on the short wave ...

What wave the voice of Monsieur, not our friend, Montand is heard on these days I don't know. You can confirm, Ferfichkin, that I don't "sit glued to the radio", I don't listen to any foreign stations, I haven't even got a radio, or rather I have, but the batteries ran out ages ago ... I do know something else though: young people these days wear jeans and T-shirts and carry bags with "Montana" written on them, but this Montana isn't the singer, but an American state whose capital is Helena, and this has got nothing at all to do with my epistles, and now I'll come back to that rogue Grandad Pasha squashing my kitten, who'd been named Myth in honour of the then darling of the public, the famous French singer Yves Montand, who was in that film *Wages of Fear*, about some working people shifting some exploding

19

gun-cotton and getting good wages for it. Yves Montand also sort of got blown up afterwards, or maybe he didn't – when *Wages of Fear* was around I was only a young kid, which makes me entitled to a bit of memory aberration and I'm not going to surrender that to anyone.

So – Grandad Pasha was a hefty man, still extremely strong for his years (in 1956 he was 75), he had a crew-cut, salt-and-pepper coloured, a good fur coat, sheep skin, in autumn he used to wear a sailor's quilted pea jacket, and in summer a tusser-silk jacket, and a Ukrainian shirt embroidered with cockerels which he wore outside his trousers, tied with a tasselled rope. And Grandad Pasha always went around in high boots, clumping about for all he was worth and never thinking to look what was under his feet.

So there's the whole saga for you. Once upon a time there was a kitten, but there isn't any more. Along came Grandad Pasha clumping his boots, not thinking to look what was under his feet – and suddenly there's no kitten. Didn't even have a chance to squeak, the kitten didn't.

"You old sod! You shit-bag! You clapped out *kulak*! You Port Arthur prick!" I whispered mentally to Grandad Pasha, looking at him with unchildlike hatred.

But Grandad Pasha just broke into a smile and said to me: "Go and see what there is in the pockets of my fur coat, I hung it up on the peg, go and see what there is in my pockets . . ."

"Grandad Pasha, why did you squash my kitten?"

"Eh? What?" Grandad Pasha finally thought to look under his feet and for some reason wasn't in the least bit bothered.

"Well, see, it was such a titchy little thing," he said, even a bit resentfully, after which he walked out of the kitchen into the room to drink tea out of a glass and vodka out of the small, blue, faceted glass.

And when I had buried the kitten by the winter rubbish dump, wept over his snowy grave, and gone back in the house, Grandad Pasha, both he and his George medals radiant, was recounting in his own words the same thing that the lyrics were all about in the song "On the Hills of Manchuria", which had just been sung with such brilliance through the amplifier on Programme One of Central Radio by People's Artiste of the USSR L.G.Zykina, of whom the poet D.A.Prigov has composed the following noteworthy lines:

> Lyudmila Zykina sings
> Of when she was seventeen.
> So what about her being seventeen?
> When she was that old she hadn't even won the
>   Lenin prize ...

But that's D.A.Prigov reflecting on a different song "The River Volga flows, and I am seventeen", for in the song "On the Hills of Manchuria", which I knew only as a waltz until it was sung on the radio through an amplifier, Zykina used to sing (in 1982) "It's quiet all around ... sleep, heroes ... the kaoliang is rustling" etcetera, and that's what Grandad Pasha was talking about at that time (1956). I remember even being scared when I listened to a People's Artiste singing like that (1982): "Isn't this song ideologically harmful? Isn't it tantamount to admiration of the imperialist policies of the former Tsarist state, on whose territory we all live now?" But I quickly calmed down, realizing in time that they would never broadcast an ideologically harmful song. Moreover, it wasn't out of the question that it was some "Family Favourites" concert and the waltz "On the Hills of Manchuria" had been requested by the mother of some

21

soldier to cheer him up while he was serving in the army. I don't know.

"In life there is always room for the heroic deed," he asserted, "but I admit that it was terrifying when we were sitting in the undergrowth of the kaoliang and the Japs were blazing away at us from all directions. Shrapnel would come whizzing over and you'd be shitting in your pants. But so what. The NCO would shout, and we'd advance. Hurrah! Hurrah! Keep your bayonet atilt, and the Japs would make a bolt for it, puttees flashing by, when you dashed down the mountain. And then you'd be making a run for it, when it was their turn to come charging down the mountain shouting 'banzai, banzai!' They had horrible faces, goofy teeth, holding Samurai swords in their hands. Then you really ran fast, because no one wants to die in vain. But I was no coward, I fought bravely. I carried my commander away on my shoulders and I saved our Russian flag, for which I received all the George medals, all classes. I even had a sabre, only they took it away from me in 1919 . . ."

"The Whites or the Reds?"

"I don't remember," Grandad Pasha would answer, taking a drink and something to eat, after which he would breathe out noisily and strike up in his croaking voice:

Where the waves of the Amur roll along,
Abraham sings his Sarah a song . .

"Uncle Pasha, did you know that Abraham and Sarah are ancient Russian names?" Mama would interrupt.

"What's that to me?" Grandad Pasha would snap back. "I've got nothing against the Jews: Jews are polite people, and if they poisoned Stalin, then they did the right thing, God rest his soul, and peace eternal to him."

"How can you say such things, Uncle Pasha, in front

of a child?" Mama would say, blushing and scowling.

"I didn't mean anything," said Grandad Pasha in conciliation. "Stalin was a fine fellow, he won the war. I understand that it was all Beria's fault, he was an English spy . . ."

Christ, Grandad Pasha really talked his head off in 1956, when he returned to his homeland from the outlying districts of the city of Ulan-Ude, where for a long time, safe and sound, he had been whiling away the time in complex reflection on the meaning of total collectivization, while cracking cedar nuts, shooting squirrels and catching fish. Yet as soon as Stalin died, Grandad Pasha immediately turned up in the city of K. accompanied by Evgenya, a brawny pock-marked woman, getting on in years, a cossack woman of the Semeisk clan from near Lake Baikal. They set up home in a little wooden house near the railway station, but they didn't have any children . . .

It turned out that during the interval between the Russo-Japanese and the First World Wars Grandad Pasha had acquired a strong passion for horses, but being just a stable hand, a poor peasant, he had no capital in sufficient quantity to satisfy his passion. Having deserted from the front of the imperialist slaughter-house as it fell apart, Grandad Pasha returned home to his native village of Amelyanovo, which, being the place of exile for the Decembrist gentry, was situated on a Siberian highroad 25 versts from the city of K. and was populated in the main by descendants of Taganrog peasants, who had moved there in the C19th on the occasion of economic reforms and developing Russian capitalism.

A rich, large village – that is what Grandad Pasha returned to from the First World War front. He came not as a foot soldier, but on horseback. And a stallion ran behind the mare.

Soon, exercising the privileges of his new authority and

possessed of extraordinary abilities, Grandad Pasha established a whole stud farm: he traded horses, went to horse fairs, got beaten up in the town of Minusinsk for professional swindling. He neither ploughed the earth nor sowed millet. Unlike his own brother Grandad Sasha, who grew real red water melons in Siberian conditions, and fed his children on them till they burst, and "pissed the bed" at night, as Aunt Ira put 50 years later when she told me about it. So by the time total collectivization began, Grandad Pasha's fate had been decided: in the dead of night he wiped out all his horses and disappeared. Grandad Pasha's brother Grandad Sasha was the village elder in Amelyanovo. He grieved deeply over Grandad Pasha and tried to sell the horse meat to the Tartars in Slobodka, but the Moslems refused to buy it, unjustly suspecting that they were being palmed off with carrion, and not slaughtered meat. Grandad Sasha had the meat and bones buried, and a lot of fringed half-length coats made out of the hides, and the horses always snorted and turned a troubled, disapproving eye whenever a citizen wearing one of those coats got in their sledge.

Oh, Grandad Pasha, Grandad Pasha! You killed the Japanese, the Germans, the horses, and then you stamped on my kitten, you old bastard! Forgive me, Grandad Pasha! You died in the autumn of 1960, and the coffin was set up on stools in the yard of the little wooden house by the railway station amid the wreaths and flowers. Brightly shone the September sun. Softly keened the widow Evgenya. The women snivelled. The menfolk frowned. I photographed the funeral with my "Smena" camera, and only these photographs will now confirm that, when I described you, not a single word was untrue. Sleep peacefully, dear Grandad Pasha! You know, if you'd stayed alive, you'd be 102 years old now, but that doesn't happen to the Russians. It's not like Abkhazia, there's a different climate here ... They've formed a folk ensemble of geriatrics in Abkhazia. The geriatrics in our country are all under the ground.

28 October 1982

GRANDAD PASHA'S BROTHER GRANDAD SASHA

was the village elder in Amelyanovo. Something happened to him. I think this will be of interest to you, Ferfichkin, and will add something to the sum total of your ideas about life.

No, what happened to him wasn't that his father, my great grandfather on my mother's side, was exiled with all his family and bags and baggage from the province of Taganrog to Siberia. I don't remember Grandad Sasha, there was about a six-year gap between my birth and his death, so Grandad Pasha used to relate how as a little kid he walked behind a cart across the whole country from the shores of the gentle Azov Sea straight to the bushy-topped cedar forests, which at that time hadn't yet been felled, into the village of Amelyanovo, where the Decembrists had lived, been pardoned, had died, having enriched the culture of the locality, and of whose bitter fate the official folklore narrator Fyokla Chichaeva sang at regional amateur art festivals. Something quite different from this happened to Grandad Sasha, but I'll come back to that later, first I'll set out on these pages a feeble little family legend.

The fact was that Tsar Alexander II finally in 1861 freed the workers and peasants from the boundless domination of the industrialists and landowners. Hurray! Down with serfdom! Down with corvée, handing over half your harvest to the landlord, quit rent, droit de seigneur! Down with serf theatres, where young actors and barbers weep from unrequited love in the guttering light of tallow candles! The inhuman hoarse shouting of "Down with" – let's all, we curly-headed lads, plough our own land, and when we've scattered "wheatee" in the barns, let's sing and dance and play the psaltery! It's possible, Ferfichkin, that that is just what the labouring people thought, for the father of Grandad Pasha and Grandad Sasha, great Grandad Danila, whom I can only picture with difficulty, began to lead a fairytale existence after the "Manifesto of 19 February": he grew stronger, he came up in the world, he turned his peasant hut into a house, he carted his crops to Taganrog, and occasionally it seriously crossed his mind to go into wholesale trade and to send his offspring to grammar school, so that they could squeeze the serf out of themselves drop by drop, just like A.P.Chekhov, also a native of the Taganrog wide open spaces, whose father, it is not entirely out of the question, great Grandad Danila could have met from time to time – on the steppe, at the market, in the church, whence the pious Pavel Egorovich dispatched his maturing sons to sing, and it's not entirely out of the question that my great grandfather stood somewhere there behind the pillar in the church and quite hypothetically he could have exchanged three kisses on Easter Sunday with Anton Pavlovich. "It's not entirely out of the question, but it's more likely to be unlikely," you'll snigger, Ferfichkin, and most probably you'll turn out to be right.

So then, my friend, great Grandad Danila, whom I can only picture with difficulty, brought his grain into town and having made a good sale, allegedly set off to celebrate his good fortune at the Tsar's Arms where he got dead drunk, but when he was settling the bill they found a forged "Katya" on him, that is, a banknote with a portrait of Catherine Alexeyevna II on it, she who conquered the

Crimea, wrote novels and was the private patron of the French writer and enlightener (mentioned in the epigraph to this book) Voltaire, François-Marie Arouet, honorary member of the Petersburg Academy of Sciences (1746).

They started shouting! Window panes were smashed! After a certain time had elapsed great Grandad Danila was dispatched together with his family to tame the virgin and fallow lands of the Siberian wide open spaces. Grandad Pasha strode behind the cart, while Grandad Sasha as a mere babe-in-arms sat with the women in the same cart. And in the hazy heat of an August noonday sun the fine city of Taganrog vanished, whence A.P.Chekhov was not watching them depart, for by that time he too had abandoned his home town and gone off to Moscow so as to busy himself with literature seriously, though for the time being only in humourous popular magazines.

Now, a little while ago, Ferfichkin, I went out of my house in Tyoply Stan to buy some Astra cigarettes, and as I was walking past "Jadran", the shop of one of our fraternal allies, I saw, in the brightly-coloured crush of multi-national Soviet people who were in the process of acquiring everything that the Yugoslavs purvey in that shop, that a Zhiguli car was boldly drawing up, behind the wheel of which sat a fool wearing a moustache, chains, trinkets, all dressed in leather and velveteen. There was a significant inscription in his windscreen, written in foreign green letters:

Tagany Rog

"Oh, you ragged sod!" I said, not knowing why I felt so resentful, as I stood by the closed tobacco kiosk, gazing forlornly around. Though in point of fact, Ferfichkin, what was wrong with that inscription? Every man strives for culture. Every man keeps pace with the times. And if it fell to me to receive greetings from the great-grandfatherland in this way, then it's God's will – contact's been made, and now I recall perfectly "Tagany Rog", through which I was travelling just a little while ago in a dirty train with its windows knocked out and its doors all battered, Taganrog, the city which my forefathers abandoned in the C19th, due to circumstances which were nobody's fault.

I won't hide the fact, Ferfichkin, I just wonder sometimes – what if my smart-operating great grandad forged that "Katya" HIMSELF, and that's why it was right and proper they packed him off to distant parts. But on second thoughts, I utterly reject this romantic version. In the first place, given the sharp depreciation of the currency and the introduction of silver monometallism, banknotes were partially abolished in Russia from 1 January 1849, in the second place, in that case great Grandad would have been transported in chains, and not to Amelyanovo to a free settlement, but to Nerchinsk-Akatui to mine ore for the country, and in the third place, our entire family has always been genetically and pathologically incapable of drawing pictures. I, for instance, am so incapable of depicting a real object that I sometimes wonder if I shouldn't take up easel painting, having breathed new life into the decrepit art of abstractionism, which has been gobbled up lock stock and barrel by pop culture. There could be a great experiment in "modernism" here, since even when I was at school, the art master Kanashenkov got furious when he saw HOW I had drawn an alarm clock that was stuck right under my nose. "What?! How can you possibly get the perspective SO wrong? How can you possibly mix up everything all at once – colour, light, line, tone?" the teacher used to lament. "Have we got a budding PSTRACTSHINIST here?" this honest-minded man (1956) would say, staring right through me, and with a sigh

28

of pity giving me a C minus, for in all other subjects I was always a star pupil.

"Have no fear, teacher, abstractionism isn't the road I went down. Your pupil grew up into a naturalistic realist, who boldly asserts that: 'GREAT GRANDAD DID NOT FORGE MONEY'".

Though he was a bit gipsy-looking, a bit Greekish to look at, as incidentally is Mama, and incidentally is our whole family, including Grandad Pasha, Grandad Sasha, Granny Marisha, Uncle Kolya, Aunt Ira, Natasha, Ksenya, Kuzmovna, Fyodor who makes musquash hats, Pyotr, Uncle Gosha's son, and Uncle Gosha himself, Ninka the thief and honest Kotya – that's on my mother's side, because as regards my father's family, that's another story: on that side, apparently, they were all mystics and boozers, you only need to look at Uncle Vanya from the city of Eniseisk – one glass of port wine and some bilberry tart and he'd be off ten to the dozen about gods and spirits . . .

Deep is time, and murky are its waters. I don't know any of my forefathers' other ancestors, the older ones are dead now, and there is no one else to ask. I don't know anything at all about any other ancestors. I don't want to lie and make things up. Or root around in the archives. Oh, you Russians! You did exist, after all, so how could the thread be broken? After all, I had great great grandfathers and great great great grandfathers, and stretching back into infinity great great great. Will anyone tell of them? Is it necessary? Is it necessary to RESURRECT one's fathers, Ferfichkin?

Blue is the tobacco smoke, and there is no answer to this question on the platform at the end of the carriage on the train going from South to North. Only the concrete pillars flashing by . . .

Aunt Ira, born in 1910, was a little girl during the Civil War, and her father Grandad Sasha, was the village elder in

Amelyanovo, and this village kept constantly "changing hands" – as, for a completely different reason, it was put by my geography teacher, a Buryat called Apollon Petrovich, who was married to a German Jewess called Rimma Borisovna, which gave rise to their having very funny children who all received a higher education and lived in Leningrad – so that, Aunt Ira always said, the peasants soon had no idea who was who. The White officers going on the rampage, saying farewell to the homeland, and cutting down the wild cherry trees with their sabres. Then came the thunder of cannon fire, and they galloped off wearing only their long-johns, but a week later they would re-enter the village, this time wearing red flashes, and again be asking for pork fat, horses and homebrewed vodka, addressing Grandad Sasha directly. Grandad looked long and hard at these misdemeanours, and then fixed himself up a dry warm nook in the cellar, and at the first signs of any threatening army on the outskirts of the village, he would go down there, put his round glasses with their wire frames on his nose and read Afanasyev's Russian fairy tales. Many a day and night he spent down there during the Civil War, and remained, in the absence of any pretenders to the position, the constant elder of the village of Amelyanovo, right up until the violent disappearance of Grandad Pasha at the dawn of total collectivization. After that, he disappeared too, moving 25 versts into the city of K., hiring himself out as a carpenter on the construction site of the Forestry Institute, which after the Second World War became the pride of Siberian science. Grandad Sasha also built a huge timber house for himself on the side, with a woodshed, a garden, a bathhouse and a vegetable plot. Just before the war he sold half this house to the future Vlasovite Nikulchinsky, while all our family lived in the other half. As I remember it now, Ferfichkin, in 1952 we came back from Karaganda and five of us together occupied a whole room of grandad's old house – me, my sister, Mama, Papa, and his mother, Granny Marina Stepanovna, a rabid anti-stalinist; in the main room lived Aunt Ira, cousin Sasha and Granny Marisha (second granny on mother's side), in the connecting room lived the lodger Anna Konstantinovna, who had contrived to return from Stalin's labour camps before his death and who knew how and when to keep her mouth shut; there were more lodgers in the kitchen behind a plywood partition, the drunkard Nikolai and his wife Elena nicknamed "Demyan". Our whole colony co-existed in a friendly, jolly atmosphere, we celebrated the revolutionary and other public holidays together, drank toasts to peace, so that there might not be war, to the homeland, to Stalin, to good relations between people, and sometimes we remembered Grandad Sasha.

And this is what happened to him. When total collectivization came to an end Grandad Sasha was a shock worker and his portrait hung on the "red board" at the construction site of the Forestry Institute. However, once when he needed to obtain some silly little document from his home town, he went the 25 versts into Amelyanovo, and it came to light that in his native village he was registered as the brother of Grandad Pasha, a runaway kulak who had slaughtered his horses, and this threatened him with serious consequences, were it not for the kindness, bordering on irresponsibility and loss of vigilance, of his fellow villagers. He was lucky, otherwise he could well have been shorter by a head, despite his high social standing as a stakhanovite, who originated from the poorest strata of Siberia's revolutionary peasantry. He was lucky ... He died a natural death in 1940 in the comfort and tranquility of his own half of the house, surrounded by kith and kin ... Ah, Grandad Sasha, Grandad Sasha! What a pity I only saw him in a photograph! He would have taught me the carpenter's

31

trade, and I too would have become a respected member of society. But it was not to be – the carpenter died six years before my birth. He was lucky, I'm not. Do you agree, Ferfichkin? ...

Today I remembered you and me discussing just what a good set they were, those people in the C19th. Dostoevsky, Leskov, Tolstoy, Mussorgsky. The young branch – Chekhov, Gorky, Kuprin, Bunin, Merezhkovsky. They led a great life. They ate well. They wrote their works. Wore starched shirtfronts ... Frockcoats ... Shaking their beards, craving for reforms, angrily protesting against ... Oh, dear country! ...

Today, Ferfichkin, is ACCUMULATION DAY. I am not writing anything today, I am just looking around, eating, just like in the C19th, and having a drink. Today I paid a visit to the artist M. and his wife A., a great poet of contemporaneity (female gender).

"The Parthenon, the temple of Athena Parthenos on the Acropolis in Athens is a marble Doric periptery with an Ionic sculptured frieze, the architects were Ictinus and Callicrates, Vth century BC; the reliefs of the metopes and the frieze are attributed to Phidias, to Phidias; the temple was partly destroyed in the XVIIth century, later partly restored, restored! ..." said the artist M., pouring drinks with a generous hand.

"Don't reject what you've got used to, even amidst occasional luxury, don't turn your nose up at the commonplace, God will punish you, you'll lose one thing, then another . . ." the artist M. was saying, eating a sprat in tomato sauce.

As if struck by thunder I peered into his inspired face, the face of a conquering hero and king of Bohemia, living his life with pride and precision. You ask me, Ferfichkin, to tell you more about these famous Muscovites, whom fate has made my friends, but I am afraid that through clumsiness I will invade some delicate area of human nature and I'll spoil everything. And anyway, I'm not used to it. Understand this, my friend, and don't be angry with me. There is absolutely nothing to get angry with me for. We ate ravioli, drank vodka, recalled friends, including you, all sorts of stories concerning you. If we ever see each other again, then I must tell you them, and they will really amuse you, because not one of them corresponds with reality.

31 October 1982

I place two old photographs on the table to help me try and understand what, for all that, my

GRANDAD EVGENY

really was.

Photo No.1. On the back is an inscription in faded violet ink:

Your Nephews:

Anatoly 5 years old
Vsevolod 8 mths old
Concordia 3 years old
and their Nurse

33

The handwriting is pleasing. The size of the photo is 9 × 14 cm. The photographic paper is portrait bromide or sepia toned unibromide (brown tint). The quality of the print is high, but apparently nothing out of the ordinary given the photographic technology of those years. You can pick out the finest details in the picture: the lace in little Concordia's shoe, the little strands of hair on young Vsevolod's forehead as he is dribbling, the iron wheel and the corkscrew grips on the handlebars of the tricycle which my future papa Anatoly, wearing soft Russian boots and with an angry expression on his face, is sitting on. *"Their nurse"* is standing behind young Vsevolod and is looking with dignity into the lens. The nurse's clothes: a black skirt, a white blouse with a lace front. Concordia is sitting on a bent wood chair, her fingers spread out. The photo was taken in the summer, outside, by a white wall, whose lower part consisted of two rows of cut logs, but it is not out of the question that the whole house was made of wood, and in order to take photograghs they had hung a sheet up to give the impression of a plastered surface. There is a cigarette end lying on the ground.

Photo No.2. Size 5.5 × 8.7 cm. The photo is pasted into a cardboard passport measuring 6.5 × 10.7 cm. At the bottom on the right hand side of the passport there is a vertical inscription in pressed gold *"I. Upatkin"* and a vignette in style moderne, which incorporates the name of the city *"Krasnoyarsk"*. The photograph depicts a man and woman standing next to each other, he is about 25, she is about 20. Not without reason, I assume them to be my grandmother and grandfather on my father's side, that is, Marina Stepanovna, the future wife of a priest and rabid anti-stalinist, and the future priest Father Evgeny. Given that I know he died in 1918, in circumstances which have yet to be elucidated, at the age of about 50, the date of Mr I. Upatkin's photograph of the young couple ought to be put at about

1893, which, by the way, would match the dress and hair style of the people: grandmother is wearing a dress with flounces and a blouse with a high, straight lace collar, like a "turtle-neck", and I can't explain how her hair is arranged, you need specialized knowledge and terminology to do that; grandfather is wearing a white, embroidered Russian shirt that fastens at the side with two buttons, and a single-breasted jacket, Grandad has a downy moustache on his upper lip and a haircut *à la* future "Beatles", pertaining to a period when *Komsomolskaya Pravda* referred to these English musicians as "beetle-shockworkers" (c. 1962). Grandfather and grandmother are nice people, it's pleasant looking at them.

I want to add to the description of Photo No.1. (the children with their nurse), and just say that it relates to 1915, for my father Anatoly was born in 1910, and on the back of the photo it says that he is 5 years old, I never saw Vsevolod or Concordia, I never heard anything about Vsevolod, but someone did sort of talk about Concordia, either Mama or Granny . . . They used to talk about her as "Aunt Conda". Consequently, in this photo at an early age there are Papa, Uncle Vsevolod-the-unknown and Aunt Conda who disappeared God knows where, and if you wrinkle your brow, Ferfichkin, then remember I'm not forcing you to read this, and I have absolutely no need of the kind of reader who wrinkles his brow enigmatically, because what I want, that's what I write, that's how I want it and how I know how to do it, so there. If you don't like my epistles, if you're bored, then go buy yourself something with a bit more of a spark in it under the counter somewhere, from Ivan Fyodorov the first Russian printer, sorrowing away in the very heart of the capital, staring with metallic eyes. So then! . . .

Now that I've described, one way or another, these two photos and put you to shame, my presumptuous Ferfichkin, you and I must resolve a string of questions.

First question. Were my ancestors on my father's side rich people? Everyone seeing that photo taken in 1915 of well-fed children, a nurse, a bike, and Russian boots, will answer this question affirmatively. And everyone, most likely, will be wrong. I don't think they were rich, but were well provided for, and that's two big differences, as they say in Odessa, a native of which city, the poet L., used to tell me about his grammar school teacher, who was not rich, but was well provided for by the size of his salary, which permitted him to wear a civil service tunic, change his starched shirts every day, rent a small three-roomed flat, and keep a cook called Dusya. But he couldn't afford an annual holiday in Nice or Yalta, he couldn't go to the theatre often and drink champagne. I think there were different criteria for wealth in those days which are practically incomprehensible to us today, for a well paid comrade today (basic wage 180 roubles, plus up to 40% in bonuses) these days cooks his food himself in a saucepan and gets the cash from God knows where to flit all round the Crimea and the Caucasus every summer. Even a poet-songster with a basic income of 50 thousand roubles a year, or some future defendant in the dock, who is at present quietly engaged in embezzlement on a massive scale, is in no position to employ a cook. And yet they're rich men even in comparison with the real former members of the bourgeoisie, whom October 1917 put paid to.

Second question. Suddenly it's crossed my mind – hang on, was Grandad Evgeny a member of a cult? Maybe it was him, and not his brother, my father's uncle, who was a White officer, and who didn't wait around for the approach of the feared Shchetinkin's proletarian units, but mounted a horse and galloped off through Khakass, Tuva, Mongolia and Manchuria to the Chinese city of Harbin. Tell me, you

36

Chinamen, there, in Harbin, have you seen my grandad? Or maybe he went even further, and founded a firm producing vodka for the western states of the USA, eh? That's all rubbish, but Granny Marina Stepanovna used to talk about a little church outside Minusinsk, and of how subsequently all its plate was removed: brocade chasubles, icon mountings, and then they did for grandad himself, but they didn't touch the actual icons, the BOARDS, as present-day black-marketeers call them ... No, it's not true – Granny never expatiated on the causes of her first husband's (Grandad's, Father Evgeny's) death, she would only say curtly: "He died". It was Uncle Vanya, the boozer, who whispered to me once in Eniseisk, looking all around from behind his official, deputy forestry director's desk, that both brothers, my grandfather and his, Uncle Vanya's father, had been pushed under the ice in 1919 near the village of Vorogovo in Krasnoyarsk region, and not at all in the south of that region where Minusinsk is situated, which again creates confusion and uncertainty, though why couldn't the two grandfathers have been transported by boat down the Enisei from Minusinsk to Vorogovo, and pushed under the ice there, where by then it would have been thicker? After all at that time there was no Krasnoyarsk hydroelectric station, and the Enisei was perfectly navigable along its whole length. Oh, no, that's stupid, why transport someone anywhere, when you can finish him off on the spot ... Nonsense, sheer nonsense ... "And who pushed them under, the Reds or the Whites?" I asked Uncle Vanya. "You guess," answered the deputy forestry director, looking around in all directions, as if expecting devils suddenly to appear which he would have to neutralize with a crucifix. And he and I carried on drinking, and at last we went out into a wide public yard on the north side of the building, where his personal chauffeur – angrily waiting for him – was sitting on a jeep, on which for days now they had been unable to make it to the remote forestry plots. Uncle Vanya threw the storehouse doors open wide. "Nephew, I want to make you a gift. Take everything you want from this storehouse . . ." But there was nothing in the "storehouse", apart from a pair of huge tarpaulin boots size 43 hanging up on a rusty nail . . . Deeply touched by his kindness, I took the boots . . . "They've got a special nylon lining, they're special lumberjack's boots, if a lumberjack cuts off a piece of timber and it falls on his leg, it won't break the bone, it'll only bruise," boasted Uncle Vanya. "Tell me, what do you think, does God exist or doesn't he?" he asked quietly, bringing his studious face close to me, the fragrant stench of raw brandy on his breath.

No, my grandfather had definitely been a priest all right.

Third question. Why do I rake over the past? *Answer*: it's interesting.

Ah, Grandad Evgeny, Grandad Evgeny! . . . It is a pity that he left this life for another so early. If only he had placed his hand, smelling of incense, on my young head, I might possibly have grown up quite different, a more moral person. And how wonderful I would have felt in church! I would have understood everything that went on there: the meaning of the icons, the rapid words of the lesson, the stage-managing of the service. But things have turned out for me so that God exists but the church doesn't . . . Well, so be it then! As they say, in the coach of the past you won't get far . . .

1 November 1982

I've been deprived of the opportunity of writing to you today, Ferfichkin, because life has hit me hard: another rejection. Yesterday I met an editor, practically an Editor-in-Chief, who smelt of French perfume and Russian mists, wearing a leather coat made in Mongolia, he was on Herzen Street standing near a Volvo, and he asked me, even a little bit slightly irritatedly: how are things with you, and when I told him that I didn't know, he instructed me to inquire at a department, where a certain "Tatyana Gerasimovna", a lady of about forty, who had the look of the Central House of Writers about her, informed me that she was forced to return "my material", for "its subject matter did not suit our journal", and this despite the fact that I had substituted the words "swine" for "fucker" and "she-devil" for "bitch". And you know, there was a time when they flattered me, Ferfichkin. I was flattered everywhere, and published almost nowhere. "So be it, there are people worse off," I thought, looking at "Tatyana Gerasimovna", but I was really upset. It's insulting, Ferfichkin, my hands are shaking . . .

2 November 1982

I had better make a formal declaration, Ferfichkin: the main point of my epistles to you is in my wanting to make a leap out of my habitual world of short gloomy prose works into the free open space of diffusion, idle chatter, non-obligation, free will. Away with poring over words and the pains taken in choosing them! . . . I couldn't give a damn for so called craftsmanship! You know that I've always written my works without considering whether they'll put food on the table or not, but even that's not the point: let reality be juxtaposed to madness, otherwise you can sink to the depths, as happened to me recently, when I found myself alone, face to face with the world, in the sea one September night on the border of Abkhazia and the Russian Republic. You are going into something, there is no moon, and there is something there in

39

front, and to the left, and the right, and behind, and above, and below – everywhere. And you forget who you are, and what, and why, and where, and when – a mad longing drives you towards dry land, whose dim night lights drawing near return you to reality, from which there is no exit. You can't mutter: "Away with despair" – for despair is unreal. To exist in despair is like swimming out into the lonely Black Sea near the River Psou on the border of Abkhazia and the Russian Republic.

All right. Forgive this insignificant digression into a private real life, this brief instant of weakness, of self-centredness, of paraliterature, for now I'm ready, and once again I come back to my original point of departure, once more I am travelling on a train, thinking about money boxes and relatives. So let me continue, Ferfichkin.

HYPOTHETICAL GREAT

ANATOLY?

EVGENY?

My name is Evgeny. My father was called Anatoly. Grandfather was Evgeny. Great grandfather was Anatoly. I don't know anything at all about him now, except that he too was a priest, like Grandfather Evgeny. Hypothetical great . . . was, probably, Evgeny as well. Or Anatoly. Great . . . is lost, like a swimmer in a lonely sea. When I heard that one of my great . . . had married a Tungus woman, an assimilated Siberian Tartar, I understood where that genetic strain running through my father's family came from: the slovenliness of our everyday behaviour, the tolerance to hard drink, by which we could drink for a long time without becoming alcoholics, at times getting drunk on small doses, at times on large doses, according to mood during a drinking bout. And that's no trifling matter, it's very important! There is

40

nothing trifling about this business of ours! A Russian and his vodka is a very important subject, only these days who is a Russian and what is vodka?

Let's rather listen to the words of Karamzin, Ferfichkin:

The battle, the last for Kuchum, lasted all day: his brother and his son, the Tsareviches Iliten and Kan, 6 princes, 10 lesser nobles, 150 of the best warriors fell under fire from our troops, who at eventide ousted the Tartars from their stronghold, drove them towards the river, drowned more than an hundred of their number and took 50 prisoners into captivity, a few escaped on vessels in the dark of the night. Thus Voyekov had his revenge on Kuchum for the death of careless Ermak! Eight wives, five sons and eight daughters of the Khan and no little wealth were left in the hands of the victor. Not knowing Kuchum's fate and thinking that, like Ermak, he had drowned in the river depths, Voyekov did not consider it advantageous to continue the journey: he burnt what he could not take with him, and with his noble-ranking prisoners, returned to Tara, and reported to Boris that in Siberia there was now no longer any Tsar other than the Russian. But Kuchum was still alive . . .

But Kuchum was still alive when my hypothetical great . . ., who had taken fright when Voyekov ". . . ordered that all the Tartar prisoners, apart from those of noble rank, be beaten and hanged", turned his bloody gaze to heaven and became a missionary, having in his entourage that slant-eyed young beauty, whose father and brothers were laid low by the powerful pressure of historical progress. Ah, great . . . Evgeny, ah, great . . . Anatoly! Why don't I know anything about them, why didn't they, like me, leave epistles to some

Ferfichkin of theirs? Look, over the course of four centuries our male family conscience would have developed something for humanity, some mystical formula for Happiness. Yet because of our laziness and inertia the world is going to die anyway, and so are we. After all, it's a fact that: shells are exploding, machine guns are crackling, planes are flying, and missiles are being launched, so we must get something more written down and pretty quick, otherwise, this is what you get:

> The escalating waste of material resources in the military sphere, the huge scale there of use of energy, of fuel and of other materials vital to the creative activity of society, result in the arms race becoming an ever more tangible brake on social progress.
>
> *Pravda*, 17.1.1982

6 November 1982

So . . . Just take a good look, Ferfichkin, at how things are. All I do is move from this table and get plugged into the mice-like scuttling of life, in order to acquire the financial means necessary for existence, and before you know it, I haven't written you anything for the last 3 days now. And now, having penned you a purely formal RECEIVING ATTENTION type letter so as to stop my conscience pricking, I am going off to a birthday celebration for a dear 50 year old acquaintance of mine, comrade N., which is the only thing occupying my thoughts at the present second: what I'm going to say to him, what he's going to say back to me, who else is going to be at the celebration, should I take a bottle. So many problems! . . . And me . . . what about me? I'll try not to get drunk, and tomorrow I'll get on a bit further, that is, I'll start telling you about my Grannies Marisha, both of them. About Granny Marisha on my father's side, Marina Stepanovna, the former priest's wife and rabid anti-stalinist. And about Granny Marisha on my mother's side, simply Granny Marisha, a pious former peasant woman, who came to live in the little town of K., where her husband Grandad Sasha built the Forestry Institute. I'll also put in somewhere there the story of how I used to steal birch wood from our neighbour Aunt Fenya and became terribly rich at the age of 15, having teamed up with a wastepaper collector who had a stall on Markin Street, although I'm afraid that this information will tarnish my bright aspect, and I will appear to you, Ferfichkin, as a man playing the role of petty swindler and degenerate of the first water, which would be, in retrospect, a distortion and a slander on the image of your contemporary, that is, on my good self, because if I really am a swindler, then I'm a big time swindler, and I'm not degenerate at all.

Here's something else I remember, Ferfichkin, among other things. Once, about 15–20 years ago when I lived in the city of K. my friend R., these days a well-known Soviet writer, was telling me about a certain person called, if I remembered his name correctly, Schwitters and showing me a quotation from a book called *Modernism Unmasked*, published in the USSR, in which the formalistic Schwitters, I don't know to this day, whether he was an artist or a poet, had the impudence to assert that he had merged with art to such an extent that even if he, a German, spat on the floor, then that would be art too. Schwitters, of course, was overdoing it, but there was something in what he said. Look out the window – there is art all around us, and maybe, if you stop any passer-by and ask him what kind of a day he's had, you'll be writing Joyce's novel *Ulysses* before you know it, though it's not out of the question that getting it printed would be, to put it mildly, a bit difficult. Take me, for instance. How have I spent the last three days? God strike me dead, I don't remember. The day before yesterday I was sort of putting together some kind of hack-work, I was in a terrible temper, chatting yesterday to the well known Soviet director F. about the success of the Soviet cinema today, and we agreed to co-author a film script for 2 thousand, if THEY ALLOWED HIM TO HAVE ME. In the evening, at a modestly, but neatly laid table (pizza, apple pie, candles, tinned salmon, cervelat and a bottle of red wine), my wife and I waited a long time for the well-known Soviet poet-guitarist E., teetotal, fastidious, avoiding crowds of people and mundane vulgarity. Shit! The bard didn't come, but he rang 3 hours later, to tell us in slurred and fading tones, that he was completely drunk and was beating his head with shame on the table at which he was still sitting. That they had got him drunk, and that he didn't dare show up at our house in that condition. "It's a pity," my wife and I said drily, hanging up. And we added: "It's a pity you're not coming, but to hell with you, you drag, we're all right with just the two of us." We drank the red wine and talked about art. We finished the red wine, finished talking about art, and went to bed. That night there was the first snow of winter. It fell imperceptibly, but by morning all the quiet earth had become white, and the yellow sun rose, and then our comrade Yu. telephoned from the Austrian city of Vienna. In a faltering, tremulous voice, he told us that everything was all right with him, that he'd been met, that he had all new clothes on, that Viennese wine was cheap and that he would soon be going to Paris. We were sincerely glad to get his call, though we poked fun at Yu., while still feeling a bit scared about talking. And the poor fellow mumbled on for a long time, sparing not a thought for the phone bill, whether it was his or someone else's. The pips. The end. So what, each to

44

his own. For one man it's knocking around Europes and Americas, for another it's writing to you, Ferfichkin, and, when he's got drunk on vodka, sounding off at his dear comrade N.'s birthday celebration, whither it's probably high time to go. Time to clean your shoes, press your trousers, tie your tie ... *Jedem das seine*, Ferfichkin, each to his own ...

I suggest you compare the two dates. My previous note was written on 6 November 1982, and that means that there is another day left separating you from my reminiscences about my Grannies Marisha. But this was no ordinary day, as the dating shows. I slept late that morning, because of a hangover caused by my being at the birthday party which I informed you of in my previous epistle. We had a good time at the birthday. There were about 20 people there. We were drinking well and eating well, dancing to the tape recorder, to various tunes on it. We were all aged between 30 and 50. We were all tired. Some got drunk, some didn't – it didn't make any difference. No one argued with any one about anything. No one agreed with anyone. About what? But, anyway, it's not important, Ferfichkin. No, I am completely satisfied with the evening spent there ...

There was, it's true, a little set-to: I gave a lady a kick up the arse, for throwing a kitten at my wife and telling her, "That's the kind of fur that suits you." The lady remained almost calm, just called me a "bastard" and added an epithet to that word which I would have been proud of, if it had been 1958 and I'd been 12 years old, but it is 1982 now, and these days I consider it almost an expletive.

And the next day was marvellous. I had a good sleep, turned on the television and saw a bald-headed comrade, the well-known novella writer Plastronov, winner of all sorts of prizes, making a speech. I looked at his good-natured face edged with reddish mutton-chop whiskers, and it occurred to me that he had gone a bit soft in the head, considered himself to be Prince Skopin-Shuisky, who was saving Russia from the sodding Poles in the Time of Troubles, though people who knew him claimed that he was a typical false pretender to the throne, grabbing everything that was going. All right, God be with him, I felt sorry for him, he would come unstuck, and end up in Kashchenko psychiatric hospital, looking mournfully out of his little springtime window. If I live to see it, I'll take him a parcel there: some yogurt, a bread roll, some Ostankino sausage at 2 roubles 90 kopecks a kilo. After all, his wife will have left him! ...

Just before lunch a couple of companions and I were strolling down a street covered with the first stubborn snow, and we got as far as Uzkoe where the church cupolas were dazzling in the rays of the first winter sun, and next to them was the former property of the Trubetskois (the former Sanatorium of the Central Commission for the Improvement of Scholars' Lives), and now the Academy of Sciences' sanatorium, where a policeman would not let us through to "view the architecture", because "You've seen the sign saying UNAUTHORISED PERSONS NOT ADMITTED" ... The mid-C18th manor house had been rebuilt at the end of the C19th, there were stables, ponds, arbours, paths, dark avenues ... Honourable members of the Academy could stroll there at their ease, but for the sake of objectivity, I must add that less learned folk also got in there from the direction of the housing estates in Yasenevo, cutting through the deserted park pathways, after all, it's impossible to fence off the whole country, there wouldn't be enough barbed wire ... They climbed over the fence and sat around on the benches drinking port wine, thus disrupting that so thoroughly thought out system of recreation and complaisant Muscovite serenity.

We turned left away from the police post and went under the golden cupolas of the Church of Anna (1698), where according to some rumours, "Goebbels' ideological archives"(?!) were kept after the Second World War, and according to others – the manuscripts of Russian religious philosophers, which had turned up there when the Institute of Philosophy was undergoing capital renovation or something. Or during the protracted inventory-taking at the main library of the same institute . . . I don't know . . . I don't know anything . . . I'm a long way removed from any kind of "philosophy". From "politics" I'm even further removed, but I've already told you that a hundred times, Ferfichkin, so I don't want to repeat myself . . . We turned left away from the police post, preserving the peace of the former estate of the Trubetskois, and I, anticipating some entertainment, took my companions to view the yellow factory-like building, built at the start of the century, near where, the last time I had been out here, there had stood a green-coloured mock-up of a field kitchen with signs in the old orthography, all in preparation apparently for making a film about that time when the workers revolted, or the First World War started, or had just finished and a new war was in progress, the Civil War, with the Russians killing each other. There was a pleasant middle-class district next to the yellow building: geraniums on the window ledges, a drunk with a concertina pestering two old women, who were sitting on a bench by the gate, cracking sunflower seeds, the words "district soviet" and a village shop with its "like it or lump it" choice of goods in short supply. The last time it had been real Italian spaghetti made of hard sorts of wheat flour. So then . . .

47

I related all this ardently to my companions, but it turned out that the first stubborn snow had covered the area churned up by bulldozers, and all that now remained of what had been here formerly was just a welded steel pyramid-shaped memorial, behind iron railings, bearing a roll call of the inhabitants of the locality who had died in action against the German-fascist invaders. I was genuinely aggrieved. I apologized to my companions and we went away from the encroaching concrete tower blocks of Yasenevo. There were three of us: me, my wife, and D.A.Prigov. Kind Dmitry Alexandrovich, in order to console me, told me that he had moved to Belyaevo from Mytnaya Street at the beginning of 1966, having lived previously in a rough and ready communal flat. He moved into a luxurious three-roomed co-operative flat. In those days everything around there was open fields, there were mushrooms growing everywhere, and berries ripening, villages and hamlets clung to the highroad, while the tower blocks were to be found only near the Belyaevo metro station, there were only three in number, and the Belyaevo metro station didn't even exist then, the last stop on the metro then was Novye Cheryomushky, so named in honour of an experimental housing estate, which had since given its name to all similar housing estates in all the large cities throughout the length and breadth of the mighty Soviet State. D.A. said that in 1966 he used to walk to Uzkoe, and in those days there were no railings around the former Central Commission for the Improvement of Scholars' Lives sanatorium, and I told him that in 1966 I was a student at the Geological Prospecting Institute and was living in a hostel on Studencheskaya Street, where I used to get drunk and get into fights, and my wife said that in 1966 she went into the 10th grade of a selective school specializing in the humanities, and they had their own theatre, and they put on A.Blok's *The Rose and the Cross*. This school was also situated on Studencheskaya Street, and we spoke a little about how we might well have met and got to know each other then, after which we went home, read poetry, and ate duck stewed with buckwheat porridge. The duck was just a touch on the fatty side, but it didn't matter, it was tasty, and we drank "Bear's Blood" wine, which was a little on the sweet side, which led me to suggest to the assembled company that it be diluted with water, as was the practice with the ancient Greeks and Evgeny Kharitonov, watched "The Blue Light", which was a bit on the boring, amorphous and tasteless side, talked about how the standard of "The Blue Light" had fallen – there was a time when the great names shone in all their glory on that programme! We were contented with our existence, just like those petty bourgeois who today lived in that district churned up by bulldozers. We knew who was who. And we ourselves were no lightweights. D.A.Prigov recited his latest fine verses, thus reminding us not for the first time that he was a poet; my wife, taking a hair of the dog that bit her, had been stubbornly working on a vaudeville called *Corrida* right up until we went for our outing; and it's all the same to me, Ferfichkin, what I am, but as you can see for yourself, I'm also working, composing epistles to you. We were feeling good because of the drink and because a friend had come to pay a visit, and the three of us were enjoying the pleasant conversation, the meal and Channel One of Central Television, while outside the window a storm was raging, having built up by the evening to become a counter-weight to the idylls of the afternoon – the sunshine, the serenity, the snowy pleasures of the countryside, but now the cream-coloured curtains at the window were drawn, and ... and forgive me, Grannies Marisha, that once again your appearance in my epistles to Ferfichkin is being post-poned. Pardon me for troubling you and don't be angry, don't be angry with me for the procrastination, stay put for just a tiny bit longer where you are now, before you make a fleeting appearance on these very pages, which your dear grandson is writing all over, using a blunt pencil, as evening draws to a close, transmogrifying into night, the very kind of night that there was many years ago, when a cannon in old Petersburg roared, proclaiming to the world the birth of a new world, different, unprecedented, wondrous, magical, fantastical, multifarious, bright, resonant, dramatic, tragic, life-affirming, wholly directed to the future, my world, your world, our world . . .

Ah, Grannies Marisha, Grannies Marisha! . . . But, you know, you didn't love me, I suddenly realize that now with extraordinary clarity. You were both completely different, and neither of you loved me. Well, let me be absolutely candid – maybe I didn't love you either, if confessing every last thing is what I am so futilely, oh so futilely, trying to do . . .

9 November 1982

I just do not understand the reason why yesterday I started whining about my two late grannies' alleged dislike for me. It was probably that habit that we are given to in our family of play-acting and clowning. Clowning and play-acting are things that everyone in our family regardless of age has always loved: me, my sister, Mama and Papa, and aunty. I don't suppose that my grandfathers and great grandfathers shunned this utterly forgivable human foible either, sometimes it develops into a talent . . . What I'd like to know is, when am I going to get fed up with spinning things out, describing a lot of old geezers who are no use to anyone, and decribing myself, equally of no use to anyone? As soon as life intervenes, it'll all come to an end ... Is that it? Is that how it's going to be? These last sentences are the crux of, not the sequel to, the clowning, and contain a perfectly reasonable question – what is literary composition, does anyone need it, how is it to be defined and is it (defining it) possible? And from the word go you cannot embark on a free flight, but must, according to the rules, take a nice clean piece of paper, describe the train to Moscow, and how someone, let's suppose a comrade of yours, or simply someone else, tells you something, and the other passengers listen, and also relate something, since they've got life stories worthy of novels, and the train goes on and on, ever deeper into the expanses of Russia. And yet it doesn't just go on, but goes on LIKE A PLOT, that is, something OF A PLOT is going on in a seperate composition. EXAMPLES: 1. The main character intends to blow the train up. 2. Detachments of Nestor Makhno's troops attack the train. 3. I am on my way to BAM. 4. A beloved girl is next to the hero in the train, he gets to know her and ... 5. A mystery play of alienation is being performed. 6. As the stories and reflections proceed SOME-THING is forming.

Emphasize the necessary, but nothing will come of the aforementioned, for I have embarked on a free flight, that is, not a flight where I kept repeating that rubbish: "flight, flight", it's bad taste, this word "flight" ... it's not a flight, but simply a ... I'm simply, you know, writing like, scrib-bling a bit. What are you writing now, Zhenya? Well, I'm writing like, scribbling a bit ... Just an ... AUTOTESTIMO-NIAL: I wouldn't say I'm sluggish and weak-willed, but withdrawn and hermetic. I once popped out into the open world and was so nicely treated to a smack in the puss with a stick, that I immediately retreated back into to my burrow behind the curtains. I don't know about others out there, but my wife and I like it here in our two-roomed co-operative flat, with the curtains drawn, and we don't like it at all out on the street, where everybody is trying to shove past you, scowling, surly, utterly alien . . .

That is why, Ferfichkin, I had to take the photographs of my RELATIVES out of the trunk – so as to recall a few things, have a think, ponder a few things. And it is not entirely out of the question that with the word "relatives" I'm implying a great deal more than . . . "Than" what? . . . Than, well, people with "biological connections". Though am I getting mixed up? Relatives are relatives and there's no getting away from them, and no reason to, because they're relatives, and if it seems to you that I've got completely mixed up, then I agree with that, for I've given the reason above: I'm withdrawn and hermetic. And if I'm too free and easy, then it's only from despair. I'm going to carry on in my own impudent fashion, without regard to anything, Ferfichkin! I want to write and I'm going to! I want to and I'm going to get cracking! . . . I've been moaning in my latest "works" that I'm tired and that I'm going down hill, but now I declare that I'm not at all tired and not at all going down hill, I'm just being pressured from all sides, that's what has made me tired. I really feel like performing some sort of function on earth, but there just isn't any fulcrum I can use . . .

Nonsense . . . The only thing I have achieved is that I write every day, even if it's only a little, just as Hemingway taught us, just before shooting himself. But this gives rise to a great many questions, to which there aren't any answers. In the first place, do you really write every day, comrade? In the second place, no one is interested in whether you write every day or if you're soon going to stop writing altogether, which would cause a good many people to heave a sigh of relief. In the third place, I like writing. I used to like writing before, too. I wrote texts. I have written texts all my life and I love doing that more than anything else in the world. I love it. Fresh violet ink in the inkwell, East German paste in the ballpoint pen, the pencil is sharpened, the typewriter is tapping away, and it's good, it's correct, it's congenial. And if I don't want to concentrate the reader's mind, distract him, lead him on, intrigue him, then that's my business, Ferfichkin. I warned you, you're free to stop reading my epistles at any page you like, but it won't change anything, for I'll bring my epistles to a logical conclusion of some sort, or bust (you, me, us).

Right, that's enough. It's time to take myself in hand and get back on the train to the grannies, grandads, uncles, aunts, sisters and brothers, though in all conscience I must say that I've got no desire at all to get out of this pleasant little lake of lazy thoughts, of fading away, of decomposition, of tepid smelly water being overgrown with weed.

Come on, friends, let's sing:

THE CHRYSANTHEMUMS IN THE GARDEN HAVE
    ONLY JUST FADED,
BUT LOVE FOR RUSSIAN LITERATURE STILL BURNS
    IN MY ACHING HEART ...

I don't know what kind of family Granny Marina Stepanovna, the mother of my father, a major who didn't make lieutenant-colonel, came from. I only know that she was the wife of my Grandad Evgeny Anatolyevich, a member of a cult. If I am not mistaken, her maiden name was Krasnopeeva, but I probably am mistaken, because that was the surname borne by her sister Felitsata Stepanovna, who suffered from glaucoma in her old age and was laid to rest in a distant village on the Angara, as a guest of her son, my Uncle Kolya (not the "home-baked milk" one, but another one, my father's cousin). This Uncle Kolya the Second, like his brother Uncle Vanya, already described in these pages in

53

his capacity as a donor of official boots, also worked in the forestry commission, he was the director of this department of the forestry commission, and he burnt his own house down as a result of carelessness. As is the custom, his mother, my great Aunt Felitsata Stepanovna Krasnopeeva, who in her thick glasses looked like James Joyce, came to the man who had lost everything in the fire. And there she was laid to rest, ashes to ashes, dust to dust, in that remote village on the Angara. Before her death she greatly loved her son, who, being a candidate of sciences at the end of the fifties, worked in the Forestry Institute, had a library at home which contained a pre-Revolutionary volume of Nadson, and also had a beautiful wife, two growing children, boys, who these days do not want to know him, because he "had acted basely". Consequently, he was no ordinary person was Uncle Kolya the Second, and since he worked in the Forestry Institute, he invented a kind of machine which, in my ignorant opinion, only an alcoholic was capable of inventing. Judge for yourselves – this machine was small, yellowy in colour, made of steel, and had arms. You applied this machine to a pine tree that was still just about standing, and like a monkey, it clasped the trunk in its steel arms, and climbed up, cutting off all the branches that got in its way with its razor-sharp blades. So that afterwards the lumber-jack in his sleeveless coat and his size 43 tarpaulin boots found himself not sawing up a tree but to all intents and purposes ready cut logs. When he invented this yellowy-coloured machine, Uncle Kolya wasn't able to get it patented for some reason, but he became extremely proud – he abandoned his beautiful wife, his children and his library, and, tempted by the allurements of a new scientific career involving the practical development of what he had already invented, he moved to the city of Chita, where they offered him a university Chair, and where, in a state of inebriation, he was soon shooting a gun at his new wife, for which he featured in a TV "Crime watch" programme. "I can imagine how ashamed he felt," his ex-wife told me, "You know, Nikolai is such a proud man ... Never mind, he'll come crawling back to me, he'll come crawling back ..." But when his son by his second wife came back home from his parachute regiment the first thing he did was give Uncle Kolya a broken arm and rib, for which he got two years under Article 206 of the Criminal Code of the Russian Republic. That's why, when he'd been patched up, Uncle Kolya decided to give up his scientific career, of which he was sick and tired, and strike out on his own, managing a forestry enterprise in a remote village on the Angara, where he set fire to his house, almost got burnt to death himself, jumped like a lion out of the window, whereupon his old mother came to the man who had lost all his possessions in the fire, and died there, far from her native Eniseisk ... My ancestry is hard work! ...

So it is hardly likely that my grandmother's maiden name was Krasnopeeva. Although ... no, hang on a bit ... That's right, it's absolutely right, my grandmother's name was Krasnopeeva, and all the Krasnopeevs in our family originally came from the northern village of Vorogovo, which is on the Enisei, near Turukhansk. Uncle Vanya's and Uncle Kolya's surname was Pustokhvalov after all, so therefore the surname Krasnopeev didn't well up in the weed-covered lake water of my brain for nothing.

Granny Marina Stepanovna Krasnopeeva-Popova-Fedoseeva also came from clerical folk, and had been to school somewhere, but I don't know where exactly. What was there there in those days? A parish school? An episcopal college? A teacher-training college? ... I know that by family situation she was a priest's wife, but at the same time she was a teacher of Russian language and literature, and held the title of People's Teacher. So when my real grand-father PASSED AWAY in 1918, she promptly married a certain Vasily Anisimovich Fedoseev, a man of simple stock, but also a teacher, who was as bald as Fantomas, and organized the Pedagogical Institute in the city of K., and died of consumption in 1937. From then on grandmother stayed a widow right up until September 1953, when she died as well, having savoured before her death six months of life without her hated Stalin. I saw the photograph of the man who was not my real grandad, Vasily Anisimovich, on a stand which depicted the founders of K.'s Pedagogical Institute, when I went there on a small matter of official business for the local branch of the Artists' Fund, for which I was then working (1972). I had come to conclude an agreement with the rector of this Pedagogical Institute, a thoroughly uncouth type, who bore the name Koreisha, the name of the famous "God's fool" of Moscow, who served as a prototype for one of Dostoevsky's characters (viz. F. Dostoevsky, The Devils, Moscow, 1957, p.749). This new Koreisha didn't conclude the agreement with me, but on the contrary just gave me a lot of filth. At first I felt like answering him back, and telling him that my grandad had founded this institute, which now paid this "God's fool" his wages, but then I changed my mind, rightly thinking that a rector like him would put a word in the right ear and settle my hash. So if this Koreisha isn't dead yet, he'll never find out what I really thought about him on that memorable day. And if he is dead, then all of them, Stalin included, have met up in heaven, and are possibly talking about us.

A People's Teacher of Russian language and literature. A school-marm. She taught Russian language and literature in school and technical college. Father (in 1928) put down on a form that he was "the son of a civil servant, of teachers". It was safe and to some extent honourable that my parents be

TEACHERS pure and simple, rather than some kind of obscurantists ... More about my father: he played football, he was called up into the army, he became part of the SYSTEM, was a major and didn't make lieutenant-colonel ... All right, it's beyond me, but thank you Vasily Anisimovich for not taking fright at a priest's wife and her kids, though she was as pretty as a picture (on the other hand).

I also know that grandmother had a lot of sisters, and they were all beautiful, even if they were original inhabitants of the region. I have a photo (tinted or bromide portrait 13 × 18 cms), with them all taken from a three-quarter view, shoulder to shoulder, there's a lot of these grannies, and they are all school-marms and priests' wives. They all have straight, close cropped hair, all wearing short jackets, white blouses and pince-nez. Ever so many grannies! All beautiful! ...

Yet why Marina Stepanovna hated Stalin in particular always remained a mystery to me, after all, he never did anything nasty to her personally. I was seven years old the year they both died and I never got round to asking granny why she honoured the leader with the designation "old foreign gob", and, shaking with anger, said to her sobbing mother on 5 March 1953: "What are you crying for? The bloody old devil has kicked the bucket, and not before time ..." I should note for the sake of objectivity that Granny Marina Stepanovna did not GENERALLY harbour antipathy towards non-Russians, she just led a secluded life behind her screen in the room, and when she died there, they even found a slim volume by the great Georgian poet Shota Rustaveli among other books in her estate ... I can't remember, did she honour the former leader with such words before his death? I can't remember. I think it's hardly likely "before" ... Her meek, hard-drinking son, an officer in the system, would hardly permit his mother such liberties ...

And anyway, Granny was not apparently one of "those who throw themselves under tanks", as the layabouts of no fixed abode in Aldan put it. The enigma of this inexplicable phenomenon of an ordinary person's hatred for the great leader still torments me to this day, and it fires my imagination with stupid, nonsensical fantasies about passive inner resistance, the masses understanding everything and so on ... I also recall hearing vague stories from my dear departed parents about how they and Granny burnt some books in a hot stove at dawn, bits of them blotted out, people's names, pictures ... Scraping, slashing, cutting ... And what if Vasily Anisimovich PASSED AWAY in precisely 1937, then he probably really did die of acute consumption, otherwise my father would not have been able to work where he did go and work afterwards ... All right, all this is apparently wide of the mark ... I've gone rambling on too much ... Look here, Evgeny Anatolyevich! ... Well, I'm just, never mind, I'm doing it for the plot ... I'd better tell you then about a perfectly ordinary man, practically a man of the people, Vasily Anisimovich Fedoseev's father, my great grandfather once removed, Anisim Sevastyanovich.

My great grandfather once removed, Anisim Sevastyanovich, really was a very ordinary person. Brought into the city of K. from the country and taken in 1936 to a travelling circus with a view to spiritual enhancement and closer acquaintance with world cultural values, he thoroughly disgraced his highly intellectual son and his daughter-in-law, my Granny Marina Stepanovna, in front of the whole town, by reacting to the performance, from his seat in the row reserved for the élite, in a fashion that was more lively and direct than that permitted by the rules of upper class, or even lower class, etiquette. He engaged the clown Mamalyga in a verbal duel, in stentorian tones, and, using highly specific terms, he censured the state of déshabillé of the ladies on the trapeze, expressed pity for the bear, the camel and the tiger, and failed to be escorted from the premises solely thanks to his grey hair, his bald patch, his highly-placed son and to the era, which respected the ordinary man for being ordinary and wise, something they even made films about. A year later Vasily Anisimovich died, and Anisim Sevastyanovich also died, but in 1953, on 5 September, Granny Marina Stepanovna died, surviving her arch enemy by exactly six months.

Oh, I remember perfectly Granny Marina Stepanovna dying. If I can remember her enemy PASSING AWAY, and being exposed for what he was at the XXth Party Congress, how can I forget the death of my own grandmother, who perhaps didn't love me very much, but was still good and kind. She coughed incessantly behind her little screen, and read books – Pushkin, Nekrasov, Tolstoy, Fet, Dostoevsky. She held no conversations with me or our folk, but women friends used to come and visit her – to whisper to each other and smoke cigarettes.

I remember being told suddenly not to go THERE behind the screen, because granny had died. They took the screen away, and a coffin appeared in the room. They put the coffin in the middle of the room, there's a photograph of that too. We are all standing behind the coffin, wearing our coats because of the cold, and looking very serious. Mama is looking sorrowful, father, as usual a bit drunk, has turned away, as if an invisible hand is choking him, my sister is a picture of incipient womanhood, and I am looking straight ahead, over-awed. Scowling.

I remember her friends squinting, bespectacled, smoking Belomor cigarettes on the porch, silent, sighing. I remember that when we lived in Karaganda and I was 2 or 3, granny boiled potatoes, carrots and beetroot in a bucket and put it all in the shed for the prisoners, which led to a denunciation that the mother of an officer in the system was showing criminal soft-heartedness, and this officer tried to justify it, by saying that his mother was a fool, but that she didn't mean any harm, and she was doing it just by chance, without any cause, but that he of course was to blame for what had happened, he couldn't deny his guilt and was profoundly sorry, and undertook to restore order in his own family, having severely drawn his mother's attention to the incorrectness of similar thoughtless actions of hers, and giving his word of honour that it would not happen again, since it was forbidden ... I remember it all. And there's a lot I would like to forget. I try. I've been successful to a large extent, but unfortunately, not completely, and I remember everything: even the snowy steppe where the kazakh pack camel galloped along, kicking out its legs, and the HEAD-QUARTERS opposite the little windows of our Finnish pre-fab, and one of Colonel Sharatov's sons who banged a nail in a kitten's ear, and was flogged by his father for it. Oh, Granny Marina Stepanovna ...

GRANNY MARISHA,
DEVOUT FORMER PEASANT WOMAN,

was very different from Marina Stepanovna ... If the spirit of enlightenment and the Dalton Plan hovered over the former priest's wife and they burnt books in the stove, then in this locality a fair number of icons were to be found in the peasants' huts, prayers were composed, eggs were painted at Easter, and the poor and beggarly lived there, of whom I remember Anfyushka-the-nun and a little old man by the name of Grandad, who used to come from the special settlement to the city of K. to beg in the streets, and upped and died without any documents on Granny's trunk. Anfyushka-the-nun used to wear an ivory and gold cross, and my cousin always used to claim that he had seen her tail.

She had come from a ransacked convent, which had existed for many years in the village called Fallen Defenders, and its inmates had gone their separate ways, wandering, begging a crust for the love of Christ, over the Siberian part of Russia, until they too were transformed, like everything around them, or they died a natural death, as Anfyushka did in her time, and as we all shall in our time, even the most politically conscious of us. Anfyushka said her prayers wearing just a sackcloth shift next to her skin, and she combed out her sparse tresses in front of a dull mirror, and I used to think that my cousin was lying when he claimed that he'd seen her tail, for my cousin, unlike me, had now become an atheist, and I, unlike him, had by now become something like, but not completely, the opposite.

10 November 1982

Granny Marisha, who also came from that same village of Amelyanovo, was the wife of Grandad Sasha, Alexander Danilovich, shock-worker and builder of the Forestry Institute that (the institute, that is) later burnt down, and after it had been rebuilt became the pride and glory of Siberian science and gave Uncle Kolya the Second, the inventor, a start in life.

Granny Marisha the Second, unlike Granny Marisha the First, was completely illiterate. Granny Marisha was beautiful (in Siberia everybody is beautiful!), classically beautiful in that severe peasant way ... etcetera. And it's true – in Siberia morals were more lax, people could live freer lives, given the robbers who comprised the original settlers, and the complete absence of serfdom throughout the entire period of time that it existed in other places. Bears wandered the streets of Siberian towns, lynxes travelled on trams, and eagles wheeled over the city of K. in competition with the aeroplanes. The local population killed predatory animals with boar-spears, sold the valuable hides to foreigners, brewed their own vodka and feared nothing. All this, as well as the powerful genetic influence of the subdued aborigines and the constant influx of new chromosomes from the other peoples of Russia, created that remarkable beauty, which led Lomonosov to declare that "the wealth of Russia will increase by means of Siberia", as we can read in slogans these days displayed on every Siberian ursine street corner, or hear every time someone somewhere makes a speech on the subject of Siberia. And even A.P.Chekhov, who was travelling further on, to Sakhalin, declared as he went through Krasnoyarsk, that on the Volga life began with vim and vigour and ended in moans, but in Siberia it is and would be the other way round . . . Chekhov was right, but so was V.I.Ulyanov-Lenin, who noted while on his way into exile in Sushenskoye at the end of the nineteenth century, that these parts were reminiscent of scenes in Switzerland. And though we've never been to Switzerland yet, these parts really do remind us of something, perhaps even Switzerland, because they are very, very, extremely beautiful, they are probably even 3–4 times more beautiful than Switzerland, which we once caught a glimpse of on the television, more beautiful and closer to our own hearts because they are – the homeland . . .

As the years went by Granny Marisha's face grew coarser, and she developed a double chin, yet she never learned to write, unlike me. Grandad Sasha the carpenter died in 1937, and she didn't re-marry, and didn't even harbour any thoughts of that nature. She harboured a little cow and a fair old number of pigs and chickens. The chickens laid their eggs and did their mess wherever they happened to be. Not very aesthetic. A yard. Cobblestones.

Grass growing through. A wooden barrel. The water in the barrel getting over-grown with weed, as in a lake, as in these epistles. Evening. Granny Marisha kneels by the icon stand. On the other side of the wall our atheistic family is having a booze-up with some heroes of the 1930s: footballers, airmen, fish-farmers. These days (this is in the mid 1950s) they are all working the devil only knows where as low-ranking managers of one sort or another. Uncle Gena is in charge of the shit-cleaners in the municipal refuse disposal trust, Uncle Sidor is the manager of the "Dynamo" stadium. A policeman caught me once when I was having a smoke on the empty winter terraces, having come "to the rink", and he took me to the police station, Uncle Sidor intervened, saying he knew my father, and afterwards spent a long time trying to convince me that people who smoke never grow up. He was wearing an old railwayman's greatcoat. There were tears in his eyes. And I was 8 years old, and the woman in the buffet had sold me two loose "Rocket" cigarettes, and I listened to Uncle Sidor and didn't believe anything he told me, only I was afraid he would split on me to my mother . . . I don't know what job Uncle Volya – a handsome man and a former sailor – had, he drove a Moskvich, everyone knew he stole things, but they'd soon put not him, but Andryusha-the-storekeeper in prison. He got involved with some rich people , and it was they who put him in prison, soon they'd all be talking about it in the yard . . .

It's strange that I've forgotten Granny Marisha the Second dying and us burying her, who was standing where, what the weather was like, and what we ate afterwards. It's galling. I can usually remember these sad scenes vividly . . . It's a pity . . .

Most likely, by that time I had left the city of K. and was studying at the S.Ordzhonikidze Moscow Geological-Prospecting Institute. When they were allotted, miles away, a huge four-roomed apartment with all mod. cons. on the 5th floor of a five-storied block with no lift, the old house built by the *kulak* shock-worker was demolished and cleared away. But Granny Marisha wasn't there by then, that I do remember.

Aunt Ira, her brother Sasha, his first wife, and then his second wife all lived there, that I do remember, though we had separated from them earlier, moved out of Grandad's house, left in 1960 when the post-war housing crisis had started to abate and we were allotted through "Papa's work" a two-roomed apartment, 18 square metres in total, on Red Army Street. Soon father died, and my sister took to "courting", and her suitors slept on the trunk in the kitchen ... In that very same year, 1960, but still in our old apartment in Grandad's house where we lived as lodgers, because when the property was being divided up nothing came our way, in that very same year, those bastard grown-ups broke open my first money box, my first shepherdess, 25 centimetres high, sitting down, with her ample skirts spread out and clasping her little round knees in her brownish little arms. Her scarlet little lips were slightly open, her little white teeth shone like pearls, and the grown-ups broke her open, and took out all my money, sod the lot of them, because, you see, there was the CURRENCY REFORM! The bastards, it's true! And they also pulled down the house on Red Army Street.

Oh, Granny Marisha, Granny Marisha! Forgive me for using a bad word in your presence, but more than that, forgive my scanty description of you and the epoch surrounding you ... Forgive me, but you're partly to blame for this. You became too absorbed in everyday life and passed through life like a silent shadow made flesh. You dug your vegetable garden, you were stingy, you used to say "thar" instead of "there", you made the sign of the cross when you hiccupped. Forgive me, Granny Marisha, I don't, I can't remember any more, I only caught a glimpse, I've forgotten, after all, there was something about you, after all Anfyushka didn't live with you for nothing, Grandad didn't die on your trunk for nothing ... No, I don't remember any more, I can't remember any more, except maybe – the picture? ...

...The picture. That cheap print behind glass that hung over Granny's wooden bed. There He stood before His entry into Jerusalem. And at the bottom, painstakingly drawn, was this biblical city with its winding and its straight little streets, its squares, both wide and narrow, its temples, shops, fountains, bridges and galleys. But perhaps this was not Jerusalem, and His entry into it at all? Though I remember the little engraved device: "Printed at the synodal press ..." And it wasn't a galley that was drawn there, but a barque setting sail for the open sea, with oarsmen wearing helmets sitting at their places. And above everything and everyone stood He and His disciples. They were standing on the mountain just before coming down into the city where He would be crucified ... "Now wasn't it called Golgotha, this mountain that they came down, but only to go up again, this time for the crucifixion?" is the sudden, frightening thought that has sprung to the barely literate mind of the man writing these lines. "No, probably not," he thinks. "No, otherwise poets and artists, ART would have certainly reflected the vertical-horizontal, philosophical-topographical symmetry, so does this mean that they're all fools, and you're the only clever one, is that it?" I ask.

"But isn't it the other way round? All the others are clever, and the only fool is you, writing me all this rubbish ... And it is all rubbish, especially the last couple of paragraphs ..." you reply to me, Ferfichkin.

Oh you, Ferfichkin! Oh you are one for irony! Let me give you a COUPLE ... of paragraphs (a specimen of idiotic repartee) ... Look, Ferfichkin, I'm producing all this self-duplicating rubbish for you, producing it mechanically, but do I know myself if I've got enough honesty and courage (impudence and cynicism) to describe the next detail of our social being, destroying as it does the lyricism of the narrative?

Of course I have, Ferfichkin! Here is the detail. I fell in love with the picture, studying it for hours, and when our relatives moved into the new apartment and the picture gathered dust behind the cupboard thanks to my growing cousin's atheistic sensibilities, I asked if I could have the picture for myself, and they gave it to me willingly. But I was soon forced to part with it again – by its nocturnal removal to the dustbins in the dark yard. There were bedbugs living in this remarkable picture, and in addition to their living presence, one could see their nests as well. I am being squeamish. But I'm a fool. All I had to do was quite simply replace the frame and the glass, once I'd sprayed the old cardboard with "Prima" aerosol beforehand. However, I knew little about life in those days and didn't even guess that such aerosols existed, for which I am being punished now by writing these perturbed lines. Goodbye, Granny Marisha the Second. Once again, I'm sorry that everything is turning out like this ...

21 November 1982

AND LIFE HAS INTERVENED, OR RATHER – DEATH,

I'm telling you excitedly, Ferfichkin, but more of that anon, for the time being we're still on the subject of literature. It turns out that today is the 21st and the last time I WORKED on my epistles to you was on the 10th. So before you can say "knife", a whole ten days of literary doingnothingness has gone by. Yet other writers, who are clever people, have been writing film scripts for the last ten days, earning 12,000 roubles or producing a short novel at the rate of 25 pages × 10 days = 250 pages: 24 pages = 10.3 author's sheets, a novel of 10.3 author's sheets increases its material capital by 300 roubles at 1 author's sheet × 10.3 = 3,900 roubles (publication in a journal) + 7,800 roubles (publication in paperback journal form), that is increasing its material capital by roughly, again, 12,000 roubles, if not more, and of course it is more, 15,600 roubles!!!

So then! And all this time I've been doing I don't know what, and that's very damaging for one's constitution . . . In my view this is turning me into a flirtatious and free and easy sort of chap. Don't you think so, Ferfichkin? . . . Just a touch free and easy, boss, don't you think? *N'est-ce pas, mon cher?* Maybe I'm going mad, Ferfichkin?

No, in fact, let's leave the jokes to one side! 10 days! TEN whole days! Even if I had written two, or let's say one, little page a day, by now I would have had a whole TEN PAGES OF TEXT!!! Which is no mean achievement for me, considering that I've always been an unprolific writer, and only now, when I'm well past thirty, have I decided at last to attain authorial fecundity and line-plenitude by means of regular, unstinting work and an honest life for the good of the State. And so, not only have I not got ten pages of text, I've actually got NOTHING at all!!! I have done NOTHING these last 10 days! 10 days in my life have disappeared FOR NOTHING (I won't say in vain). And the ruin of me is that I am still studying life. I study, I study, and one asks why do I study it? I've been in Kalinin (formerly Tver), in Dmitrov, Moscow region (formerly Dmitrov, Moscow province), on Red Square, Moscow (formerly Red Square, Moscow) . . .

What's the use of studying this life, it's been studied enough, inside out and backwards, there no place left alive ... You need to work, not study. Produce pages, and multiply them. Multiply your wealth, or else you'll die one fine day, and then what will be left of you for other people, you dead fool? Sweet sod all, and burdock will grow over you, and you'll still be studying, studying ...

The only justification for my inactivity might be that LIFE HAS INTERVENED, or rather, DEATH, that in the last 10 days of my life and in the life of my country SUCH IMPORT-ANT DEVELOPMENTS have taken place, that I, as an eye witness, simply must describe them, in so far as I happened to be an immediate witness to them, and in fact even a participant. So there is a work front, there is something to describe, and I hope that I will be able not only to catch up, but to overtake myself, just like Münchhausen.

For these days it's down with laziness, down with Oblo-movism, down with the plush divan! New times are on the way, and , having called it quits with the old times, it's not completely out of the question, I shall be able to, in all probability, plunge into them boldly and constructively, swimming like a dolphin in a sea of Narzan mineral water. Today is 21 November. It's come about that in order to cover my debts I must write 22 pages today, or 11 pages (as the barest minimum). And then I'll catch up with myself, I'll overtake myself, and pull myself out of the swamp by my hair.

In an old book it is written: there is a time to gather and a time to cast away. Today it's a time to gather, and what happens tomorrow – I don't know.

But I'm not going to write 22 pages today, or 11, because in 20 minutes it will be 12 o'clock midnight and 21 November will come to an end, of which fact, as a man henceforth entrained on the rails of honesty, I simply must apprise you, Ferfichkin. It looks as if it's already striking 12. So I'll finish my writing tomorrow, after all, there's another day tomorrow. I'll write the lot tomorrow! Strange as it may seem, my debt hasn't grown at all, and has even decreased a tiny bit, because at the very, very least I have completed today's ALLOTTED TASK, at the very, very least I have scribbled one little page, so it's come about that my debt has decreased to 20 or 10 (the barest minimum) pages. I OWE you, Ferfichkin, exactly 20 pages. No, it's not 20 any more, but a tiny bit less. The chiming of the Kremlin bells, the singing of the Soviet national anthem on the radio on Programme One, and I'm already on to my second page. Is this perhaps what they call paraliterature? I know, I've read ... But I couldn't give a damn! I've rambled on so wildly and can't manage a coherent account of events, because I'm so worked up – after all, in actual fact in my life, and in the life of all the people important developments have taken place. HE WHO ONCE WAS has died.

22 November 1982

He died on the morning of 10 November, but we only found out the next day at exactly 11 o'clock. People said that he didn't die in the morning but during the night in his sleep, but as always happens in similar epoch-making cases, any event gets so overgrown with rumours, that you don't know whether to believe them or not, which fact I emphasize in particular, for my epistles to Ferfichkin are of a private, peaceable nature and are not in pursuit of political, ideological, religious or any other aims. And they are even far removed from literature, these epistles of mine, and similarly far removed in turn from real life. They are altogether far removed from everything, just as I am myself. Take a

69

look, Ferfichkin – there he is, me, right next to you, but actually I'm not here, not anywhere. I am no one, which is how I want to stay, in my homeland, nice and cosy, with the curtains drawn, or out in the kitchen, with the gas burning to keep me warm, because there's a draught from the window and the central heating is terrible. And though such improper use of the gas in the kitchen is most strictly prohibited by the rules of economy, where are you to go if there's a draught, there's nowhere to escape from, to put it figuratively, the wind of the epoch . . . I won't be mistaken if I say that soon they'll put up the price of domestic gas, and it'll be right if they put it up, because I'm not the only smart operator doing this, and there isn't enough of anything for everybody in our country . . .

However, arguing about prices is none of my business. My business is writing to you, Ferfichkin. Here I am, writing, writing, writing, and only when I've written 1000 pages in my own hand, will I call it a day and my hand will write no more. After which I'll produce a fair copy of these manuscript pages on the typewriter, tidying up the phraseology here and there, polishing up the style, refining the ideas in it, and here and there making a monstrosity of all the foregoing. That will be some work of literature! . . . If I can write exactly one page a day, then the first draft will take me:

1000	365
730	roughly 2.74 years, that is

2700
2555

1450
1460

70

2 years 9 months plus typing up at 10 pages a day:
1000 ÷ 10 = 100 days, that is

$$100 \enclose{longdiv}{}\ 30$$

$$\underline{90}\ |\ 3.3\ \text{mons., that is}$$

$$10$$

3 months 9 days, and allow 21 days for checking, and retyping in 3 copies and for a second checking – 2 months. That is, in sum, in 2 years 9 mons. + 3 mons. 9 days + 21 days + 2 mons., in 3 years and 3 months I, "If I'm Still Alive", shall make your day with my epistles. For example, today is 22 November 1982, and that means that IF I'm S.A. and God's World is S.A., then on the 22 February 1986, on the eve of the Day of the Soviet Army and Navy, I shall make your day, Ferfichkin, if of course, I don't pack in this absurd scribbling once and for all, irrevocably, "halfway to the moon", today, right now. Do you understand, my friend, that the date of my triumph would be significantly hastened, if I wrote 2 pages a day, but I know that that is not going to happen, because that has never happened to me, so why should it now? And on top of that I have no idea what else to write about. I had a plan, but I lost it. I had a scheme, but life intervened, or rather death. I'm still 70 manuscript pages short, and everything is falling apart. At the outset I was sort of travelling on a train, and recalling the story of my life. It was the Tuapse-Moscow express, but it could have been diverted to other places: Krasnoyarsk, Kalinin (formerly Tver), Voronezh, Minusinsk, Chicago, Mars, the year 1937. But you're not going to travel 1000 pages on a train whose destination is unknown, and soon I'm going to run out of relatives and there'll be no one left to describe, for other people are even worse than relatives, and as far as the plot is concerned, what the hell do I need them for?

Let's suppose that now I describe in every detail how HE WHO ONCE WAS died, and then what? Then – emptiness. Since for the 18 years of his public activity everything proceeded along a well-trodden and ever more firmly established path, and now what? ... My one remaining hope is that life will toss my way so many plots that I will have to fulfill my daily work norm 2,3,4,5 times over! I'll describe my own relatives, and other people, I'll put in all sorts of stories, in short, just you watch, I'll get out of it somehow ...

Because, Ferfichkin, I'm definitely going to complete these epistles to you, I. I'm S.A., no matter how absurd and unreadable they may be. And if there is nothing at all to describe or it is completely PROHIBITED, then I'll go out on to Kaluzhskoe Highway on the other side of the Moscow ring road and start describing all the people I meet there. I MUST finish these epistles, but why – I don't even know myself. "We're not playing for money, we've only eternity to spend ..." Everybody thought that I was joking when I was going on and on with complete sincerity in my earlier PUBLISHABLE stories about ardent love for the graphomaniac, I have never joked and I don't know how to joke. There's a simple proof of this: I HAVE BECOME A GRAPHOMANIAC MYSELF and now I'm going to gobble up the miles to PUT THE FINISHING TOUCHES TO IT, to seek out the PRECISE epithets, IMAGES, SITUATIONS ... That'll do, I've done more than enough seeking ... But I haven't lost my temper, just gone away – far, far away. Not to Switzerland or the Austrian city of Vienna, and not to Svidrigailov's America, but it's quite simple – I am not here and that's all there is to it! ... It's all the same to me what you think of this, Ferfichkin, only is it some NEW kind of WAVE? Or a NEW sort of NOVEL, eh? Well, I know it's not a "wave", I know it's not a "novel" ... "It's really, really new, like Popov's name to you", is something I've heard already, I know, and I don't care: I write without practically any clowning around, though I'd really like to.

So then. I'll now try to reconstruct the chain of events in chronological order.

On 10 November 1982, in the morning, I wrote what you've already read, or have not read, if, after the first few unprepossessing pages, you refused to become further acquainted with my naturalistic epistles. I took a bath, and having a beard, gave myself a trim with my Dutch razor with its two self-adjusting blades, massaged my cheeks with the last of my French "**after shave**", ate a hearty breakfast, and prepared to GO TO TOWN, that is – go to work and loaf about. Just before going out, at 10:55, I had a light-hearted telephone conversation with A., a great poet of contemporaneity (female gender). We were talking about life going on, or asking whether it was going on at all? Perhaps it wasn't going on at all? And about who and what were living how and where, and how who was feeling these days. During the course of the conversation we agreed that "I'd ring her or she'd ring me" – either to arrange to meet some time, or for no reason at all, I can't remember now.

I put down the phone, put on my coat, opened the door, stepped over the threshhold, and heard on Programme One on the radio in the kitchen a most sombre voice announcing something important. I went into the kitchen still wearing my coat, listened closely, and gasped. History! . . . I rang my wife at work, but her phone, as always, was engaged, – the work phone was used for personal calls too. I rang A. I shouted: "Have you heard?" – "Who?", she shouted back. "HE WHO ONCE WAS," I shouted. We agreed immediately that "she'd ring me or I'd ring her" – either to arrange to meet some time, or for no reason at all, I can't remember

73

now, but the fact of the matter was: we met that very day a few hours later ... More on that later, everything in its own time, Ferfichkin ...

I took the metro, I could see by people's faces that Moscow was calm, and many still had no inkling. That would all come afterwards: the thirsting after a miracle, the morbid hungering after spectacles, the Christian sorrow – that would all come afterwards, everything in its own time etcetera ...

At work people were already talking about it. What, and how, and why ... We bought some three-star Armenian cognac, drank to the repose of the deceased, and I went off to see the artist M. and the poet A., where we also had a drop to drink, split three ways a bottle of "Belo Stono" Yugoslav white wine ... A. said that to her my phone call had been historic, because it was from me that she had learnt that HE WHO ONCE WAS had died, even though just before that old Vanya the lavatory man with the dove-blue boozer's hooter had dropped by and said that someone important was dead, but who it was exactly, no one knew ... We ate a bit of cabbage soup. After which A. and M. went off to some reception which there hadn't been time to cancel on the occasion of our nationwide grief, while I continued on my way round Moscow.

Wait a minute! Just look what tricks the human memory plays! Altogether 10 days have gone by, and I've got the most important thing mixed up ... You see, it wasn't the 10th when they announced the death, but the day after, that is, the 11th. All that's been described above really did take place, but it took place on the 11th, but with one small exception – I wrote nothing in the morning, as the dating of my text testifies. In the morning I planned on going in to work to arrange a business trip. I woke up, took a bath, gave myself a trim with my Dutch razor with its two self-adjusting blades, which the playwright Bruegel had given me, massaged my cheeks with the last of my French "**after shave**" and prepared to go to town. Just before going out, at 10:55 I REALLY did have a conversation on the phone with the poet A. And the question arises, could I really have had time to write anything, if at 10:59 I was already ready to go "outside", as they used to add in the old days whenever, in the darkness of provincial cinemas, they shouted out the surname of someone in the audience, because he had to attend to something or for no particular reason. Let me note in parentheses that (this practice must be a leftover among the common people from the now defunct times of the labour camps, when the guards said to the prisoner "outside" and added "bring your things with you") ... But that has no bearing at all now on my epistles, and well, maybe the remark is a bit stupid ... Sorry ...

I walked along Povarskaya Street, and saw the flags already hung out, red with black ribbons, and on the road I met a lady who always informed me of what was going on in the place which I'd been chucked out of three and a half years before, and into which they hadn't re-instated me, even though they had kept promising to, well, I've got no regrets. Why have any regrets when life is on the move and is leaving the place where it once was ... The lady told me that bald Plastronov had really let himself go, was behaving tactlessly, and causing general displeasure, and I retorted that in medical science paranoia and schizophrenia are incompatible, but by no means mutually exclusive. The lady exulted at my words, and had already opened her mouth wide with meaning to inform me of something or other, when there suddenly appeared and walked past us on the street, giving me a wink and signalling an invitation for us to have a chat, E. my literary brother-in-misfortune, or fortune, if such you consider our joint expulsion from that place which they chucked us both out of on the very same day and at the very same hour. A glow of mystery emanated from him . . . The lady was about to dash up to E., but the latter pulled a face that denoted he was in a terrible rush because of business, and disappeared into one of Moscow's little yellow courtyards, leading to the former estate of Prince S.S.Gagarin, where a skinny bronze proletarian gazed intelligently from his pedestal at the yellow house, built by the architect D. I.Gilardi in 1820. The lady then asked how things were with me, and on receiving the reply "same as always", tossed her curly-headed bonce craftily, and hinted vaguely that, eh, well, maybe NOW they would look up somehow. "How come?" I asked in surprise. "Oh-ho!" she replied, wagging a devil-may-care little finger at me, but she couldn't restrain herself, and informed me that Plastronov, for example, was recently suggesting that a new article be included in the Criminal Code, as if there weren't enough in the Code already, and was criticizing pop music for corrupting the people, and Alla Pugacheva as a representative of this corruption . . .

"Oh, that prize-winner of yours will really land himself in it," I said, angrily. "Fancy that nit having it in for Alla Pugacheva, the favourite of broad sections of society! Pulling the wool over the eyes of the bosses, and creating a pretence of frienzied activity, like some lazy guard dog. He's always frightening people, always, but then suddenly, one day, they won't be scared, just like Lev Tolstoy, and then that'll put paid to your Plastronov . . . Perhaps, like Konstantin Leontyev, he wants to freeze Russia, and so go down in history, but at least Konstantin Leontyev was in his right mind, even if it was a reactionary mind, as we can read in an encyclopaedia, but this fellow is round the twist and is using his official insanity for his own personal ends . . . Oh, he'll really land himself in it! It's 1982 outside, yet he's still stuck in the mud ... But I don't hate him. I'm too far removed. I could be in outer space and looking at him through a telescope or a microscope ..."

"Yes, yes, yes," said the lady in agreement, without listening to me. "I earn 120, and a job came up which paid 150, and he took someone from outside. He offended me, very, very deeply, and I'll never forgive him for that, the bureaucrat. He's got everyone's back up. He offends people who fought at the front ... He's had himself a place built in Peredelkino ... He was practically booed off the stage at a meeting ... Even M.Kh. told him: 'That's enough of the hysterics.' He leant over the rostrum, his bald head shining, and said: 'Who said that?' 'I did,' answered M.Kh. 'And you a Hero of Socialist Labour, how can you?' 'I can, because I am a Hero,' answered M.Kh. And bear in mind that this was BEFORE ... But I implore you ... not a word to anyone ..."

"About what?"

"About what I've just told you."

"And what have you just told me?"

The lady brought her bulging, agitated eyes close to me, but by then my literary brother E., my litbro, standing by the pedestal in the former Gagarin estate, was sending me powerful signals, and I left my informer.

We got into a VAZ 2105, drove into Trubnikovsky Lane, towards the "October" cinema, and there, with the engine turned off, smoked for a long time, exchanging stereotyped, feeble-minded phrases, of the kind that millions of our fellow citizens were evidently uttering on that day. We said: "Something's going to happen", "Of course, it's not going to be like yesterday", and "We don't know what it's going to be like, but it would be nice if everything turned out okay". My litbro E. looked tired, very tired.

My litbro E. went off on his own business, and I continued

on my way around Moscow. By that time every single street was hung with mourning red calico, and in Pushkin Square near to the constructivist *Izvestiya* building a huge queue was standing to buy the evening edition with its black-edged portrait photograph. I bought 2 copies and went over to Kolobovsky Lane, to a basement studio full of sculptures, the premises of Nefed Nefedych, an old bachelor. Nefed Nefedych was glad of the visit. At first he was terribly excited, and kept running out into the kitchen to make sure the tea kettle hadn't boiled dry, but then he relaxed, squatted down, and flicked the fleas out of the fur of Kissinger, his beloved cat, and, as I recall, I even thought, I'm sorry to say, that he was excited "as if putting it on" in a manner quite incomprehensible to me. However, he was still a veteran of the labour camps, even though he had been rehabilitated, and even though he had been a party member since 1961. Now Nefed Nefedych seemed sort of enigmatic – not so much that he was at a loss, but he just turned a bit cool, and you could tell that he had no particular comment to make . . . he didn't want to.

We started talking about good and evil. Nefed Nefedych complained about the moral decline of modern youth. He had brought a 19–year-old girl back to his studio, having lured her off the street with his bohemian life-style. Firstly, it turned out that she didn't have any knickers on, and secondly, she laughingly informed him that she had only been married a month, and she was deeply in love with her husband, a student. And Nefed Nefedych could have married her as well, if he divorced his own wife, whom he hadn't lived with for many years. That debauched girl could have become his Laura: Nefed Nefedych had put his teeth in, his studio was nice and clean, he'd been commissioned for 700 roubles to sculpt two seals playing ball. Shameless hussy, said Nefed Nefedych angrily.

·I too shook my head sternly: moral standards had fallen, after which we began talking again about HIM WHO ONCE WAS. Nefed Nefedych looked vacant, and I remembered that the poet A. had gone over to the window of her garret, also stared into the distance over the black rooftops of Moscow, and the people in the metro or out on the streets had been calm, self-assured, assured of their epoch-making ordinariness, and their faces, you know ... Well, I don't know, but later, on the television ... Otherwise their faces were assured ... Does the word combination "it's all the same" have the right to exist? In the present situation? No? Yes? ... For the first time in the last 30 years something like this ... is it shock? ... curiosity? ... longing?.

Ugh! It's a stormy night outside, and it's time to go to sleep, my pen's falling out of my hand, and there is a great deal that I can't possibly convey adequately to you, Ferfichkin, due to circumstances which are nobody's fault. So then! ... How much paper, a scarce commodity, I've used up, but I still haven't been able to stride through even one day of historical events, and there's been five of them. Oh, I'm falling asleep, ah, I'm nodding off, and the pen falling out of my hand isn't falling to the ground according to the law of gravity, but is floating, floating, flying away ... The pen might have wings, and now it's flying away, flying, melting, elting, ing, ng ... There's no pen, and there'll be no me. "I'm off, I'll take 300 ether valerian drops and I'll forget myself in sleep," – this was how the character in M.Bulgakov put it. The materialistic secret of an object flying away fantastically like this apparently resides in the fact that BEFORE I used to write in the mornings, having had an excellent sleep and a hearty breakfast, but now there's a stormy night outside, and the night's no time for speaking, writing and thinking about ... Ah, the unknown German, Schwitters, has ruined me, he's ruined a poor Russian, with the lights

79

out I can't see a damn thing! . . . Aren't there any new ways of writing works of art? Using pen and paper all the time is awfully weird.

I'll try and keep my free and easy garrulity in check somehow, that's why I'm going to make every effort, suppress my own vital nature made flesh, and become immediately cool, reserved and precise. Having paid a visit to Nefed Nefedych and met there a man from my part of the world, the playwright B., I went off to see my litbro E., as we'd arranged, and there, in conversation, polished off 2 out of 3 bottles of "Areni" wine . . . My litbro bucked up.

Comments were passed, forecasts were made, there was summing up, there were resumés, things were acknowledged and things were denied. And of course there were rumours, rumours. I'm telling you, rumours . . . flew around mourning Moscow like birds. They said that both HE WHO ONCE WAS and THIS ONE had died. The son (daughter) of a THIRD had defected to America (Canada), and that a FOURTH had died, yet so as not to disconcert the people, they weren't saying anything yet, the time wasn't right, about them all having died. The trouble you get with these rumours, Ferfichkin! . . .

When we'd drunk the wine, we set off for distant Chertanovo to go to a birthday party at a lady's place, she was a child of the '60s whose husband, from whom she was divorced, was to be found in the city of Paris, a captive of bourgeois ideology, while she herself, like a little dove, pined away here in her homeland, in Chertanovo, being the owner of a co-operative apartment whose mortgage was paid off. We were greeted by: a motley and merry group of people, headed by two men of the '60s U. and Yu., delicious food, abundant booze, and the hostess herself, who was very glad of our visit, even though she ticked me off quietly for always getting into various scrapes, and for example quarrelling with the outstanding writer Zh. I told her the truth, which was that I PERSONALLY had not quarrelled with the outstanding writer Zh., my litbro E. made light of the matter, and we started eating and drinking. The third bottle of "Areni" was in my bag.

There was no table laid as such. I just can't stand this so-called "Western" way of having a party, where you all stand around in corners or sit in separate chairs eating and drinking, holding plates in your hands with knives and forks slipping off them onto the floor. Maybe I'm at fault, but in situations like that I get covered in sweat, and I always knock something over or bump into something. At the house of the fairy story writer S., I smashed a pane when I sat down on a chair by the window, and the host had to do a smart job with some coloured insulation tape to stick it all back again, which made it look like the dawn sun coming up. So then! ... Those're my views on parties *à la fourchette*! What sort of a person am I! Quoth the Raven, 'Nevermore'. I'm not at all straightforward, Ferfichkin! I have my own views on every issue! I adore myself, ha-ha-ha! ... I am a raven! I am an infantile thing of evil! ... Etcetera ...

Man of the '60s Yu. was and is a famous dramatist. He told me that he had written, published and had staged 21 plays, that he was burnt out, tired and didn't know what he was living for, and that he was not allowed to travel abroad. That THEY had said that to him – You, they said, can go on living if you like, you can publish what you like, but you're NOT ALLOWED ABROAD. I looked at him, and thought that he wasn't a bad person, and he probably had a lot of money, if he'd had so many plays on the stage. I wondered what he did with it. After all he was single, his wife had long since been living in Paris (What did all these people need Paris for!). Shameful thoughts! Counting other people's money is the worst thing you can do ... Yu. said that he'd had a phone call from America and it was very cold there. "And why don't you ever ring me?" he asked. "Never have the time," I answered, and I wasn't lying.

Man of the '60s U. kept all the more silent, getting slowly drunk and twitching his ginger boatswain's moustache. He had been a member of the party since 1963 and was a well-known writer of books for teenagers. In as far as I knew him, he was always quiet on the whole, or just asked dejectedly: "Well, how are things then? Bad, I suppose?" He listened with apparent attention to the reply, but still kept quiet, not believing you at all if you told him that things were fine and all was well. He kept quiet: previously he used always to walk round the Central House of Writers carrying a bulging briefcase, which contained manuscripts, a half-litre, and carrots from the greengrocer's. He'd come up to you and ask: "Where's Vasya?" And if you said that he wasn't around, he'd shake his head and say dejectedly: "Well, how are things?" And if Vasya was in the vicinity, he'd go up to him, shake him by the hand, stand to one side, twitch his ginger boatswain's moustache, and keep quiet. Oh, those men of the '60s! Eh, Ferfichkin?!

The lady whose birthday it was got completely drunk, completely languid, but not at all unpleasant. She hugged everyone and called them all "boys, boys ..." She had a steady boyfriend with a damn great beard. His name was Firs. I thought he was a blackmarketeer, but maybe not, anyway he had plenty of cash. He declared that he didn't want a word spoken about books in his presence, and that he didn't read them, but later on he exhibited obvious erudition and knowledge, which made me realize that his initial abruptness was only a party piece. There were also men and women there and all sorts of youngsters, but I didn't know any of them and didn't get to know them, so I can't say anything good, or anything bad, or anything at all about them, and I don't want to. It was after 3 o'clock in the morning when we made our way home. In the car U. and Yu. livened up, and started complaining that their lives were over and had run into the sand like water. My litbro E. played them a cassette of a Leningrad punk rock group called "The Pigs", and they listened closely in incomprehension and timidity to the brutal obscenities being belched out by these talented young people . . . And after that I got out of the car and headed for home, so I can't say how these complaints by the men of the '60s about life and their encounter with the new art ended, for I don't know, and in all honesty, I don't want to know, though I feel no malice towards these chaps, Ferfichkin, there's no reason to. It occurs to me now and again that they're all in the same racket, but this opinion is, apparently, incorrect and superficial . . .

I woke up in the morning with, of course, a hangover, but remembered in time the Georgian saying: "Have a drink in the morning and you'll be free all day", so I poured myself a glass of "Areni" from the third bottle, and w nt back to bed to watch television. After a little while there   as an announcement that we had a NEW LEADER. I imme iately rang my litbro E. to communicate to him this remarkable bit of news, but at the very same second he was trying to ring me, so we were able to regale each other with this fresh information only after a certain period of time . . .

Ugh! . . . Why do I tell lies and keep missing the point like this? Why is human memory so feeble? God, in fact this (the fresh information) happened the following day, on Saturday 13 November, and not on Friday the 12th, when I woke up with a hangover. Having decided to write badly, I've made no mean progress in suspiciously short time – altogether 10 days have gone by, and I'm already getting everything mixed up. So what will it be like in a month's time, or 2 months, or a year, or 10 years IF I'm S.A.? . . . No, I must keep writing, faster, faster, I must toil away stubbornly, I must get everything written down, before I forget anything . . . Write, write it down, get it confirmed, establish it in the memory, memory, memory . . . Who, what is memory? Who, what is memory. Whom, what, for me memory is . . . Oh, God! . . .

12 December 1982

Well then, Ferfichkin, another two weeks have passed since I last took up my pen. It's terrible! . . . I've neglected you, oh my pages so dear to my heart! Oh, how I've neglected you! And I've missed you so much, Lord help me, but there again, that's life, Ferfichkin. It doesn't burst in, it enchants and intrigues. As soon as life starts to play it's pipe, let all and sundry leave their homes and dance to its tune . . . I'm no exception, and indeed there can't be any exceptions. So humble yourself once and for all, humble man, and on your way, if you're able, but know that your epistolary duties to Ferfichkin have grown again. Take a look at the first date in your "work" – 25 October. And today is 12 December. So, according to the obligations that you have taken on yourself of "no day without a page", you should have written according to your barest minimum: 7 pages in October; 30 pages in November; 12 pages in December: sum total $7 + 30 + 12 = 49$ pages, and altogether we've got only 34 (in manuscript). Trouble and blatant slacking at the front! The shortfall of 15 pages must be made good and covered as a matter of urgency! By shock work! Irrespective of everything and everybody! Or otherwise there'll be total collapse, for the projected 1000 author's sheets will be raised Christ knows how high, that is, to nowhere, and that means temptation, a hassle, enticement, a game of "life and death" etcetera. Make up the shortfall right away, before it's gone for good! Before the élan has gone! Work by day, by night, don't be lazy, no lounging around! ... Overfulfil the plan by 1% by the New Year. That is 49 pages (as per the plan) + 19 pages (according to the number of days left till the end of the year) = 68 pages (the plan), and overfulfilling this plan by 1%, I must write additionally 68 ÷ 100 = 0.68 pages. So by the end of the year I must write 68.68 pages. And I will write it, since I've got 34 already (I've just got on to the 35th now), and if there's 18–19 days left to the end of the year, then there's no two ways about it, I must work, by day, by night, don't be lazy, no lounging about, write exactly 2 pages a day, and then you'll even overfulfil the planned overfulfil-ment of the plan, and on New Year's night 1983, you can formally approve a NEW PLAN, which will have arisen as a result of my initiative at work, to be precise – 2 pages a day, which will mean that the work will be finished even much sooner than was originally planned and planned again, and then you can have a complete rest, as was once suggested to Uncle Vanya, not my Uncle Vanya from Eniseisk, but A.P. Chekhov's *Uncle Vanya*, forgive me, Ferfichkin, for the poor quality of this pun – "even the brown Finnish cliff I address with a quip" (D.Minaev).

And now, my dear friend, inspired by my own decisions, I'm going to beaver away without a break, and I'll only stop I. I'm S.A. on the night of 31 December 1982 to 1 January 1983. I'll stop, I'll have a smoke, I'll have a drink, I'll give what I've written a firm, definitive appairaisal, and above all, in the New Year I'll part company with my sorrowful activities of writing epistles to you, for these labours have brought me and my home to nothing but rack and ruin. In actual fact, what the hell did I need all this for, when as a result, all I get is trouble, clips round the ear, rude signs and disrespect from the realist school? I've had enough, it's time to shut up shop, it's time to take up something more useful: car mechanics, so that when I've passed my driving test, I'll have a really relevant trade, or plant out a garden, or sow a vegetable patch, where the beetroot will grow cheek by jowl with the carrots, and the coriander with the swedes, or I'll go on a package tour to Bulgaria or the sourceless, salty Lake of Issyk-Kul, which is situated in the Soviet Socialist Republic of Kirghizia at an altitude of 1608 metres.

There are a lot of interesting things in life, but I shall continue my sad story concerning the historical events that occurred in Moscow about a month ago, on account of which I am obliged to take myself in hand immediately, for were I not to, History, The People, I and you, Ferfichkin, would all be left without my description of them.

On Friday 12 November I woke up with a hangover, my wife was at work, and I drank the rest of the "Areni" wine, after which I lay in bed staring dully at the television, on which they were playing exclusively classical music, occasionally interrupted by monotonous funeral announcements. My wife came home towards evening, and we had a row. This storm in a tea cup measured about 4 points on the Popov scale, where 10 points equals night, gloom, fog and frost, and one point is a slight grimace. Naturally I don't remember what we argued about, and I'm afraid to ask my wife, since she probably can't remember either, we've argued twice more since then – once it measured 3 points, and the second time it measured 8.5 points, because 10 is extremely serious. After 10 points the ship goes straight to the bottom, though the crew, for the most part, manage to swim for it, and get picked up by other vessels ... Though it does happen now and then that they drown ... In the first place, she won't remember, and in the second place, she might take offence, because women, like fallow deer, are quick to take offence, and whoever doesn't know that already will find out sooner or later. So on 12 November I was in bed all day long, and friends kept ringing up to discuss with me in restrained tones the sad historical tidings, and to ask what I thought about it all. How do I know what I think! So I told them that I didn't think anything, and only that I was looking at everything with wide open eyes, and recommending that they do the same, and also that today I was not answering questions, but posing them, and therefore I asked my friends: "Well, what do you reckon?" But my friends were afraid of speaking on the phone and were unable to make any intelligible reply. Or in fact didn't reckon anything, or didn't want to share their sensational information with a drunken recluse like me.

On 13 November, the Saturday, I woke up with a hangover again, but a slight one this time, and for some reason this day escapes me completely. I remember I didn't have a hair of the dog that bit me, I just lay in bed and watched television ... There wasn't a day that day, and that's all there is to it! ... I went out, bought some rolls and sausage, had some tea and marmalade ... Then the television again, and the funeral music again and some footage from the State Film Archive ...

Ay-ay-ay ..., well there you are then! ... How can you forget something like that? You'd have to be completely off your head to forget something like that! Because, it was precisely on 13 November, in the afternoon, that they announced the election of a NEW LEADER, of which fact I informed my litbro E. on the phone, while he in turn informed me of exactly the same. Away with misery, away with woe! We are reaching a new level of energy! Let's forget all past offences and discord!

I remember, I was highly, greatly excited, and now, with the passage of 30 days and nights, I'm even slightly ashamed that for some reason I forgot on exactly what day it was that I heard that important fact.

I don't want to exaggerate and say that I immediately felt, at that precise second, an influx of new strength, I don't want to tell lies, but I have some justification: it's only because the weather in November was unusually bad, and it's the same now. Take today for example, 12 December – Paramon the Martyr's day, and the Rev. Akaky's, Nektarin Pechersky's, tomorrow is the 26th Week after Pentecost. Day of the First Voice. Day of St. Andrew, the First-named Apostle, and the thermometer reads +5°C, and the snow has melted again, which means chaos for Russia, for at this time her forests really ought to be decked in their austere winter finery, the frozen fir-trees sprinkled with snow, the black twigs staring into the sky, and you boldly pulling your felt boots on. And there was the same thawing slush then on 13 November when we were informed of the NEW LEADER and on the 15 November when they buried HIM WHO ONCE WAS. Am I really to blame? And by the way, am I being blasphemous? I don't think so – it's true what they say: Render unto God what is God's and unto Caesar what is Caesar's, I don't think I'm being blasphemous, and if I'm wrong, then forgive me, Lord, and all you others who think that I'm not right.

So an influx of new strength on exactly that day, at precisely that second, was not something that I felt for the time being, but on 14 November, first thing in the morning, once again I set off to wander round Moscow, I wandered around till very late at night, and my funereal wanderings, I can say without any false modesty, became HISTORICAL, for, taking full responsibility for my words, I contend that NONE of my friends, pals, acquaintances or relatives was, on that day, in such close proximity to the place where the body of HIM WHO ONCE WAS lay in state, a place which engaged the eyes and thoughts of the whole country, the whole world, the whole planet, so that it won't be a great exaggeration if I say that I, a little man, have never been so close geographically to the epicentre of world history as I was on that sad unforgettable day. I, or to be more precise, we: I, Evgeny Anatolyevich, and a man who has already figured in these pages, a member of the Artists' Union of the USSR and former conceptualist, Dmitry Alexandrovich Prigov, sculptor, poet, dramatist, prose writer, a true, many-sided Renaissance man, who enjoyed great respect in society also because he called everybody, even small children, by name and patronymic – Evgeny Anatolyevich, Svetlana Anatolyevna, Felix Fyodosevich, – Dmitry Alexandrovich, with whom I swore, as we sat on a bench by the Bolshoi Theatre, where the "gays" used to gather in the evenings in the 1960s, together with him I swore NOT TO FORGET ALL THIS, just like Herzen and Ogaryov on the Sparrow Hills, which Prigov has depicted in his poems and pictures, while I, out of indolence and drunkenness, have fallen behind, and am only now feverishly making up the lost ground.

But that happened in the evening, whereas in the morning of that historic 14 November, the fourth day after the sad historic event had taken place, I set off wandering around Moscow, to get the scent of life and death in the air, to ask questions without answering any, and to look with wide open eyes.

And suddenly I found myself in a pub by Kiev Station, where the beer costs 50 kopecks a mug, which is a bit on the steep side for me, as I only earn a bit more than a hundred roubles a month. And it was a bit steep for my friend K., famed throughout Moscow, a former philosopher, with whom we drank beer, and of course discussed the fleeting moment.

"Well, K.," I said, "as a bald-headed prize-winning author whom you know, comrade short-prose writer Plastronov, says of himself, you are a 'politician of mean standing'. Tell me what you think. After all, during those years of your official activity in your position as a philosopher, you used to know a good many clever people, who to this very day, I dare say, are performing the menial but noble task of giving shape to arrogant ideas and directives."

"No," replied K. without even a second's hesitation, blowing the foam off his beer. "No, I don't have any grounds for making recommendations, and let me say simply, just to be on the safe side, that the LIBERTÉ gang that live round AEROPORT metro station, shouting their eulogizing assertions yesterday when they were all drunk, just make me want to laugh. I am prepared to acknowledge all that I've heard, allowing a 20 to 80% margin of error, but the fact is that subjectivity was, and is, unable to prevail in the objective world, thus my prognosis is as follows: there'll be sterility, efficiency, discipline, and austerity measures, and coupled with this, idle chatter will recede into the background, whilst still playing a significant part. 'Order' is what we will write on our schedules, and as a result the ideologists, economists, sociologists and technocrats will acquire greater significance and corresponding weight in society. The course steered will be towards practicalities, it will be a slow, smooth entry into realism, with all the concomitant consequences that that involves and gives rise to ..."

"So your prognosis is very optimistic, then! Why did you scare me to start with?" I exclaimed.

"Yes, THAT is my prognosis, I don't know whether it's optimistic or merely realistic, but that's what I forecast," said K. with a smile, niggardly as a soldier. "Because I'm a believer. I believe in God and dialectics. I'm telling you, this is an epoch-making event, no two ways about it, and you and I understand it all, and we look to the future with faith and hope, but all the same, better NOT STICK YOUR NECK OUT, for it's better that way. Remember what the late Yu.V. Trifonov wrote in *The House on the Embankment* – DON'T STICK YOUR NECK OUT . . ."

The argument was taking an interesting turn. We finished our beer and lit cigarettes. There were a lot of people in the pub, and everybody was talking about one and the same thing, and there were no drunks there. How come? Had people perhaps, figuratively speaking, started to sobre up? We went out into the street and went our separate ways, highly satisfied with one another. K. set off to tend to his own ordinary, everyday affairs, of which people knew nothing, though evil tongues had it that he quite simply used to go off somewhere and drink himself into a stupour, and I made my way on foot over Borodinsky Bridge, and was soon standing at the main entrance of the block of co-operative flats where my litbro E. lived.

13 December 1982

Here's a thought: it's silly, Ferfichkin, when ideology counts on literature and takes its seriously. You see, literature is fragile, tender, and when it can't take the strain, it breaks, it withers, but afterwards it sprouts again just the same, having grown maliciously strong on the blows and pricks it has suffered, and this makes it dangerous, insolent and poisonous. Why such a bad tradition? Let the minstrel blow away on his stupid pipe. You must understand that he is only dangerous when you pay attention to him, reckoning him to be a real force. And yet he is weakness incarnate. That is, it's not out of the question that people seduced by his immodest singing will dance round in a ring after him, but in theory it's so unlikely, in practice it's so rare, that it is not at all expedient to pay any great attention to these benighted souls, in so doing you'd only be expending a lot of nervous energy, money and human resources, and achieving totally negative results in the process. It's not at all expedient, advantageous or good. The economic system must be economical, as HE WHO ONCE WAS used to say.

22 December 1982

Look, please – It's not that I'm falling into despair, there's no despair, because life is always on the move and doesn't stay in one place, it's just that I'm so far behind this fast-flowing life, that I'm actually feeling a bit cheerful. I realize, Fer-fichkin, that you're terribly fed up with my innumerate arithmetical calculations, but today is 22 December, the shortest day of the year, but in my attempts to describe reality I simply cannot cross the boundary of that other day, that historic day, which occurred more than a month ago, and this makes me feel alarmed, confused and fearful in my soul. And this is how it always is with me: sometimes I'll run ahead of time, sometimes I'll fall behind, but I can never succeed in keeping pace with it, even if I bust a gut trying, and this give me no peace of mind, no majestic bearing, no cool-headedness, nothing . . .

I'm interrupting myself, like a dog who's had a tin can tied to its tail by some hooligans. I was describing the day of the 14 November, I wanted to tell you that, when I had drunk the beer, I was crossing Borodinsky Bridge, which decked out in mourning flags, but suddenly I introduced some incorrect, confused thought about ideology and its interrelationship with literature, and then once again I started wittering on about my not writing enough. Whatever is all this?!

No! That's enough! The time of "official whitewashing", the time of dismay, and of lack of initiative has gone! Now there must be ever-increasing concentration of energies, efficiency, a good enterprising spirit, and effective initiative. So I am finally taking myself in hand, concentrating all my remaining will power, like sour clotted milk before it becomes homemade cottage cheese, I'm deploying all my feeble technology, breaking out the reserves, so that I'll still fulfil the plan 101% by the New Year, having received from the Lord Almighty a progressive piece-rate bonus according to the results of my labour, in the form of a good mood for the coming year, appeasement, tranquility, freedom, a feeling that life isn't lived for nothing, and that there is still something to live for in the future, still something to look forward to, somewhere to aim for, that the world hasn't come to an end, that we are all going to live for a long, long time and we're not going to die one day, that blessings will rain down on every single one of us without exception, and that a sole surviving wolf will come out on to the noisy street and break into an embarrassed smile, the gap-toothed smile hiding its ugly yellow teeth, and the bright blue, that is to say, the azure, will prevail along with the yellow sunlight, so that pimples on the body will perish, and music will strike up, and the authorities will soften their hearts and release the film *Fellini Satyricon*, and mortally dangerous realistic squabbles will cease, retreating to within the realm of the family, as permitted by Freud, and tragedy will become drama, horror – comedy, and my voice will become full-blooded, not enfeebled, and it will be possible to think of fading away in a dignified manner, of the changing of life's

93

strata, of going back to nature, back to the earth, of human remains being absorbed by the surrounding roots of grass and trees, of the immortality of the soul, and of the fact that all people, as brothers, will start to worry about one another, and will forget about elbowing each other out of the way, and a diamond age will dawn, and flesh will unite with spirit, new forms of carnisoul will be established, new species will take root, and yes, yes, we'll all be happy, happy, happy. Come on, at last let's all BE HAPPY, come on, let's all forget our differences and direct our newly released energies to the common defense against DARKNESS, against the devil, entropy, disappearing. And if we do disappear, then let it be done in such a way that somehow simultaneously we still remain. Come on, let's, eh? I'm ready for it. I'm ready to become brother to anyone who throws a glance, even if it's only rarely, in the direction of happiness, peace and tranquility.

But heavy is the burden of the past and it's difficult to shake the dust off your feet right away. Your head might start spinning and you might be sick, if you find yourself in the azure quicker than you're supposed to, for the human vestibular apparatus is weak! That's why I am quietly going to continue my labours in accordance with my original "aspirations" (do you like this word, Ferfichkin?), and I'll carry on interrupting myself, because I'm producing the meat, strengthening the flesh, I'm hauling the clay, yet who is going to fashion anything out of this clay, I – don't know. Maybe me, maybe not. And, isn't all that I do just arrogance anyway?

Maybe it is arrogance as well, but before proceeding to a further elegant and severe account, permit me, Ferfichkin, at the end of the day to indulge in one good-for-nothing, derisive, filthy little thought that I, as one of God's vibrant creatures, perhaps HAVE THE RIGHT to write badly and just anyhow, like V.Kataev's MAUVISTE, after all they DINNA pay monEE for rIting, just the opposite even, they insult you, like the nihilists used to insult the God's fool, yet still you want, you want to read mEE ... See, you've read this far, Ferfichkin, so some other person would too. So why, people ask, do I keep on trying, through hell and high water, to find a precise little word that sounds good, damn it? Like Flaubert, Sterne, Babel, Zoshchenko, Nabokov etcetera right through to the afore-mentioned Kataev ... You see, citizens, I have travelled a long path of artistic creativity. At first I was a little kid, I ran to fetch the boss's beer, then I became an apprentice: they trained me, paid me nothing, gave me a thick ear, but there was no begrudging it, that's what good instruction costs. And now that I have learnt my trade, now that I've started my own work, why should I be pushed around, tormented, pestered, kept on short rations, kicked about? And, you know, it's not just that they DINNA pay yer, they shove you around, the unscrupulous swine! As if they don't understand that something rotten, even in its native soil, is dust, decay and mould, whereas something that's been preserved is seed corn, it provides growth, it nourishes, we'll all be well fed, we'll all wear clean shirts, and be clean ourselves and cheerful ... There's no need to shove me around! It's not nice! Anyhow, how are you going to order me to live my life, if for the time being I'm still alive? Will you perhaps order me to become a hack writer and to start writing really badly, if I'm not allowed to write well? What do you think? Do you think I'm talking nonsense? No, it's not nonsense. After all, now that a new, indefatigable life has begun, every worker is needed, every bit helps, as they say. So let's live, there's been enough dying, give us work that we can set our hands, minds and hearts to. You won't do anything for the cause with slogans alone, as we were rightly told from high up on the platform. When I've boldly rolled my sleeves up I MUST fulfil my plan 101% by 1 January 1983 and climb a small hill from which, possibly, new horizons will open to me. I refuse to write badly, and let that be my small contribution to the common cause. In short, the aims are clear and the tasks are defined, so let's get to work, Ferfichkin! . . . Though I have some doubts – what if suddenly everything I have crumbles away, and I'm left like a fool with sweet fanny adams for my pains, surrounded by broken bits and pieces?

CONTINUATION OF THE DESCRIPTION

of the historic events which occurred in Moscow about a month ago and evoked responses throughout the whole world (now it's MORE than a month ago, since 19 December, the birthday of HIM WHO ONCE WAS, saw the passing of precisely forty Orthodox days from the moment of his death).

Sorrow. Nation. Nationwide. People all worked up. Nothing but conversations. Once. Forev. People agitated. Grief. Fear. Curiosity. Longing.

But

DEATH HAVING VANQUISHED DEATH

Are these the right words? Am I blaspheming? On the grounds of my small volume of theological knowledge, forgive me, Lord, if I say something wrong, and all you others who consider that I am not right, forgive me too, for I am sincere. Especially as there were services for the repose of the dead throughout all the Orthodox churches on the day of the death of HIM WHO ONCE WAS, and for the fortieth day remembrance too. Throughout all the Orthodox churches . . . But what about in the mosques? The Roman Catholic churches? The Protestant churches? The synagogues? The Christian Baptists' houses officially licensed for prayer meetings? Can we cope with that question or should it be left open? Mosques, Roman Catholic churches, Protestant churches, synagogues, officially licensed houses for prayer meetings of the Christian Baptists – how many altogether, maybe a lot more? And still there's some room somewhere. A little orchestra. Funeral music plays, and plays again. Vivaldi. Mozart. J.-S.Bach. A red banner trimmed with mourning black. Borodinsky Bridge – below, the grey water of the Moscow river. Borodino, Smolensk, Berezina – retreat in the Empire style. The Russians in Europe. The first liberals. The birth of Decembrism. The Senate Square . . . Nerchinsk . . . History. So listen to this music, the music of History!

When I had crossed Borodinsky Bridge, with the "tower block" of the Ministry of Foreign Affairs and the ancient Arbat in front of me, I popped into the "Baker's" opposite the "Orbit" store, next to one of the two symmetrically situated blocks which comprise the "Belgrade" hard currency hotel, in which, of an evening, the whisky and gin flow in rivers, while the tonic water and the champagne fizz. I called in at the request of my litbro E. to buy a little bread, of both the white and black varieties.

And here I was standing at the main entrance of that block of co-operative flats, where he lives. And then I was inside this block.

We put our arms round each other. My litbro, his wife and child were about to set off for the dacha in the forest, in a good residential estate not far from Moscow, which they had rented the previous summer. My litbro's son, little Olesh, was blazing away with a toy pistol that reaked of caps. He let me have a go, I liked it. We drank tea and had some very tasty fruit conserve with it, I think it was cornel cherry. We talked about the same old thing still. Our speech contained a great many kind words and a great many good wishes, words of farewell. My litbro inclined towards the view that ... I also inclined towards the same thing. It started to rain. If it did rain or not I can't remember exactly. But that there was no sunshine I can confirm firmly, because it was overcast. A late autumn wind beat at the window, and bare slippery boughs swayed about, mourning. A black bird circled and flew past. It will fly past and circle again. On the television screen. Later. At the time, when ... It's bad in autumn! You don't notice that your summer strength is draining away like water into sand, which means that by the New Year you'll certainly be down with flu. And then what good's the Christmas tree to you, or the candles, the pie, the cheerful mugs wearing masks, if you're blowing your nose and coughing as if you were in hospital. No, take care of yourself, comrade, in advance! Wrap a scarf round your throat, mind you don't breathe in any germ-filled air, and then in the New Year you'll find living significantly easier ... My litbro looked at me "with a sharp little eye" ...

My litbro and his family set off. I stood there, watching the left indicator of the car wink mysteriously, and something made me feel quite sad. I hunched up, turned up the collar of my coat, and began striding along the Arbat to the poet A.'s place, for on that day I had to see and know EVERYTHING.

And, of course, there was wine there, how could you manage without wine on a day like this? Cheap red wine, which had got a bit more expensive either in 1980 or 1981. It's okay when there's a lot of bottles. Pour it in a tumbler – it sparkles ... (Steady now, don't get worked up, it's only a lyrical digression). Of course we talked about ... (No, it's still nice drinking wine!). Of course, we talked about how ... (Wine – that's nice!). Of course we talked about how it meant ... "Let's drink the wine," said the artist M.

"What?" I asked. "Yes," said the poet. "People are saying a lot of things," I added.

THE POET A. (inspired). He ought to ring us up and say: "I've heard you're clever people, and I would like to approach you before making any decisions." And we'd say to him in reply: "Please come over. We've got some wine, a clean glass, a plate, knife, fork, a place for you." And he'd come over, he'd have a drink and something to eat, and we'd hold a genteel conversation with him. And then he'd push his plate away, refuse to have any more to drink, on account of things he had to attend to, but we'd just carry on drinking. Then, at last he'd ask – well, what do you think? And we'd give a firm, well-thought-out answer, – in the first place, in the second place, in the third place, in the fourth place. There's this and this and this. And then in the New Year, in spring, at a time when in the old days the ice used to break on the rivers, but it doesn't break any more, seeing as the rivers don't freeze over, then, in spring, like a conquering hero he'll stride over the Earth's globe. Any simple farmer will take off his straw hat to him, the millionaire will take the cigar out of his mouth, and extend his hand to him. The forces of evil will be put to shame, and a firm, reliable stable life will be established all over the world. And prosperity.

(Her pure voice, a voice for writing poetry, the music of explosion and breaking which seeks out a head-spinning harmony at a conjunction of mysterious vocabulary and the simplest objects of the surrounding realism. I'm clumsy, Ferfichkin, I'm stupid, coarse, but THIS I can feel, and forgive me, if I've got something wrong again.)

When we had nearly finished drinking the wine, D.A. Prigov finally arrived, but he hardly drinks spirits, which means that he is hardly at all offended when someone drinks without him.

99

He had a little bit to eat from a plate and said:

"

....

.... "

I beg your pardon, Ferfichkin, this isn't at all censored smooth talk, it's just that, to put it plain and simple, I can't remember what D.A.Prigov said when he'd had a little bit to eat from the plate. I do remember how he spoke. He spoke with his glasses flashing. But what he said, I don't remember. I do remember what he spoke about. About the same old thing. About the fact that you yourself, you know, understand . . . but what PRECISELY he said, I don't remember. The spirit soared – the spirit of knowledge, alarm, curiosity, HISTORICITY, as EVERYBODY's did, and Dmitry Alexandrovich and I spoke of this when at last we left the poet A.'s place, having replied "To wander" to the question from the artist M. "Where to?" . . .

And the wayward thrill of historicity chilled the soul of the patriot, though he dissembled it behind an affected show of bravado . . .

THEN WE WENT OUT INTO THE STREET,

and it was already getting dusky, because it was autumn, it was getting dark, winter was just around the corner, soon it would be New Year, up to 22 December the days would grow shorter and shorter, and only afterwards start lengthening, and warming up, reaching the bright June dawn of 22 June, – when the Germans attacked us, treacherously breaking their promises – after which they would shorten again, and that's the way it would be throughout life.

Well then, mourning is mourning. The evening streets were filling up with people, but the ambience was so decorous, correct and well organized, that I can make so bold as to describe it realistically, without fear that someone will misunderstand me and promptly accuse me of something. At this juncture I am such a ... positive person, aren't I? Or an honest one ... I don't know, I don't know ... I'm describing how we walked along the Arbat, where A.Bely and A.Pushkin once lived (nos. 55 and 53), passing those buildings created by Panyushev, Filatov and Tryndin (51, 35, 27) which once pulled the money in, past the Vakhtangov Theatre and the "Prague" restaurant (nos. 26, 2).

Oh, my Arbat, my "rabad" (suburb, outskirts – *Arabic*), Smolensk Road, along which they built a great many buildings in the "Empire" style in the 1st half of the C19th, most of which came the way of the commercial bourgeoisie in the second half of the same century. Oh "The Prague", the golden "Prague", where people have been flocking for a good hundred years now, and still cannot get a drink of the wine they have there, nor get to eat any of the restaurant's food supplies. Oh, Arbat Square, where in 1935 the architect L.A.Teplitsky built a metro station in the shape of a five-pointed star, and the writer, Ark. Gaidar depicted the structure of this building as a symbol of ALARM in his remarkable short novel *The Drummer's Fate*, which I was discussing on the evening of 17 November 1980 on the premises of the All-Russian Theatrical Society's restaurant with the late Evgeny Kharitonov,* and we both admired

---

Author's footnote: E.V.Kharitonov (1941–1981), remarkable Russian writer. Died of a heart attack in Pushkin Street in the city of Moscow. He was born and grew up in Siberia, graduated from the All-Union State Institute of Cinematography, defended his candidate's dissertation, to which he attached no significance whatsoever. He lived on a pauper's salary as the manager of a theatre group, to which he likewise attached no significance. Throughout his entire life he was unable to publish a single line of his own works. He died, and anyone who was left in Moscow came to his funeral. Bright be his memory and to him eternal peace!

that masterly scene in which the boy wakes up and suddenly sees the yellow light swaying about on the building site in the night, and he imagines the scary words "scrape-scrape peg leg", the words SLEEP-SLEEP-HUSH-HUSH-HEAR-HEAR ... we were speaking exactly one day before we were all paid a visit by those stern plainclothes art lovers ... Anyway, it doesn't matter ... Ah, the Arbat ...

We walked through the underpass on to Suvorovsky (formerly Nikitsky) Boulevard and drew close to the House of Journalists. I used to go into that building, I used to, I used to go into a lot of buildings ... Anyway, just so it will be easier for you, Ferfichkin, to understand the geography of our funereal wanderings, perhaps I'll just draw you a crude sketch map.

There, on Suvorovsky Boulevard, in block no.6 there once lived in communal flat no.5 a comrade of mine from the institute, Sergei P., a great guy with red hair, a Jew, chatterbox and drunkard. His wife, a cross-eyed beauty called Galka, worked at Mosfilm, editing films for I don't know what. He eventually divorced her, since they fought like cat and dog till they drew blood. The story of their divorce is simple: he set up a pal of his to be her fancy man, and then he "caught" them at it, and that's why he divorced her. In 1968 me and my comrade B.E.Trosh drank six bottles of Cuban white rum at his place which he had laid in by way of a present for friends in Chukotka, in Anadyr, where he had done his geological survey fieldwork. To start with, Sergei P. didn't want to give us any rum and pleaded with us to go thirds on a bottle of Moskovskaya vodka, seeing that in those days it only cost 2 roubles 87 kopecks, but we resolutely left our lectures at the Moscow Geological Institute grasping our comrade by the arms so that he wouldn't escape. We crossed Manezhnaya (now 50 Years of October) Square and came out on to Vozdvizhenka (Kalininsky Prospect), insisting that we HAD to drink his rum, that he was OBLIGED to give it to us, since he was a drunkard and our friend, and if he REALLY did have rum at his place, and that if he really DID HAVE Cuban white Bacardi rum in his gloomy room in communal apartment no.5 in block no.6 on Suvorovsky Boulevard, then that rum DEFINITELY, ABSOLUTELY HAD TO BE DRUNK BY US. Defeated by the incontrovertible logic of our purposeful disquisitions the geology student Sergei P. none the less continued to put up a feeble resistence, and as we were going past the Garrison department store (Kalininsky Prospect, block no.10; built 1912–1913 by the architect S.B.Zalessky as a shop for the Economic Society of the officers of Moscow military command), he made a feeble attempt to dash into the shop to buy the aforementioned half litre of Moskovskaya at his own expense. But his foray was not crowned with success, and head hung, the lad suggested to us that we obtain a few lemons from a stall, "because Cuban rum goes well with 'nikolashka' – finely sliced lemon, sprinked with granulated sugar, dissolved completely in the juice that has been formed from slicing the lemon." ... B.E.Trosh and I acknowledged that our comrade's suggestion corresponded with reality and we effected the purchase, accompanying it with gestures and words that belonged to the student humour of the mid 1960s, when there was "The Jolly Wits' Club" on television, and there was ... Okudzh ... Evtush ... Voznesensk ... Luzhn ... All that was part of me, it was, it was, and I'm repeating myself, repeating myself, repeating myself, but I couldn't give a damn, give a damn, give a damn about it ...

THE WANDERINGS OF EVGENY ANATOLYEVICH
AND DMITRY ALEXANDROVICH

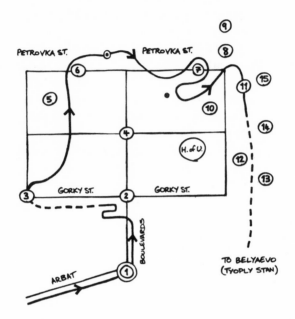

KEY:

➤ surface wanderings of Evgeny Anatolyevich and Dmitry Alexandrovich

--- subterranean wanderings of Evgeny Anatolyevich and Dmitry Alexandrovich

1 – Arbat Square; 2 – Pushkin Square; 3 – Mayakovsky Square;
4 – "Russia" cinema; 5 – Hermitage Garden; 6 – Petrovka 38;
7 – Bolshoi Theatre; 8 – Metropol Hotel; 9 – Dzerzhinsky Square;
10 – Sverdlov Square metro station; 11 – Revolution Square metro station; 12 – Hotel Moskva; 13 – Kremlin; 14 – Cathedral of St Basil the Blessed (Pokrovsky Cathedral); 15 – GUM; ● – halt at Teodor's:
◉ – Nefed Nefedych

104

"But just let me warn you beforehand that we're only going to drink one bottle," said Sergei P., opening this bottle and simultaneously boasting to us that their courtyard on the Arbat was depicted in V.Aksyonov's much talked of story "A Starry Ticket" (Moscow journal *Youth*, 1961, nos.6, 7).

"No, we'll drink all six bottles," said B.E.Trosh and I.

When we'd knocked back a glass each, we all started having a good talk. This is how I was dressed in those days: cotton Texas trousers – 5 roubles, tourist boots "Czechoslovakia" – 9 roubles, a turned "styled" jacket made of dyed officer's material with white buttons – price unknown. My comrades were richer than me, not like now, when I've decided to buy a second-hand Zaporozhets car.

"Where's Galka?" asked B.E.Trosh.

"Galka's at work," replied Sergei P.

And he poured us a second glass, but that bottle wasn't enough for us all to have a second faceted tumbler each, and Sergei P. leapt up from the table.

"Ah, play 'ccordian, play!" he howled, reaching for a fresh bottle.

Once again we poured it out, once again we had a drink, once again we started having a good talk. In part, we criticized our Komsomol organizer S. Ivanov for drinking too much and quite recently, when he was sent shopping, he'd gone astray and fallen down face first on the asphalt ...

... Radiant, Galka came home from work. Sergei P. went pale and hid the sixth bottle under the table, where its five empty friends were already languishing.

"All right, I can see you're drinking," said Galka condescendingly. "Pour me some out too," she said.

Sergei P. (his actual surname was Pauker) poured her some under the table. Galka took a drink, breathed out, ate some "nikolashka", and after a second's pause, suddenly howled, and took aim at her husband's eyes with her long, female, manicured nails:

"Right, you sod, drunk all that rum, have you?! We were supposed to have sent that to Chukotka!! We haven't got any money!"

"Be quiet, you bitch," said Sergei P. with a wry smile.

B.E.Trosh and I bid our hosts a hearty farewell and went off back to our hostel, which to this day is situated on Studencheskaya Street near the Studencheskaya metro station, to sleep . . . On the way B.E.Trosh had a fight with a professional Moscow thief. They fought in the metro, and I delighted in their duel, keeping a vigilant look out in case a policeman suddenly appeared and came over to us. When we got out into the street the thief became much distressed and, trying to wipe the blood from his face, called a taxi, only then informing us that he was a thief by profession and that this would be detrimental to his work. And that he'd get it in the neck from his wife. And that he was married and had two charming little children . . .

The next day Sergei P. did not come to the institute, but when he did eventually come to the institute, his mug bore the marks of the scratching it had received – dry, red stripes, and the Komsomol organizer S.Ivanov congratulated his comrade caustically on this fact, and suggested that Sergei P. had been punished by his Jewish God for laughing at him (the Komsomol organizer). Sergei P. didn't even reply to the effect that the Jewish God had nothing to do with the Komsomol. Sergei P. was quiet. Sergei P. once told me that in block no.7 on Suvorovsky Boulevard, where Gogol burnt the second part of *Dead Souls*, in the '50s of our century there was a communal flat, and in the famous room there with its fireplace, whose flames once greedily devoured those brilliant pages, there lived one of Sergei P.'s comrades from his childhood, just like our very own Seryozha, a boy "from a simple family". And at that time there was still single-sex education, and the boy's school, where according to the law, our dear little terrors were supposed to study, was already over full, and since the district was a fashionable one and children of senior managers lived there with their parents, there was no way that the school could take any more pupils, and so our young rebels were assigned to a school for the educationally subnormal, where there were spare places, and where the little ones pursued their studies until 1953, being outstanding pupils and yet not turning into blackmarketeers on the Arbat, as they were fully entitled to do, having suffered because of the cult of personality.

But when Sergei P. (I don't know the biography of Sergei P.'s childhood comrade, but I suspect that he is the same drunk who once turned up with him at an "old friends reunion" at the "Valdai" *pirozhki* café and fell asleep right at the table), but when Sergei P. transferred to an ordinary school, his work deteriorated and he began to behave badly. At puberty he was a hooligan, however he improved and even started at the Geological Institute, from where he was promptly ejected for poor marks and truancy, despite the fact that he coped magnificently with science, when he bothered to attend classes even minimally, for he had innate talent. They threw him out, and he worked for a year on the Taimyr peninsular, bringing back first-rate references, so he was accepted back in again and was in our group, in which B.E.Trosh and I were already studying, but B.E.Trosh and I graduated, which was not at all the case with our friend! And all because he broke his leg at his own birthday party . . .

. . . birthday party, at which he danced the *Cracovienne* on the parquet floor in the communal apartment at the address on Suvorovsky Boulevard, no.6, apartment no.5, and he suddenly fell over, cursing and swearing, saying that his leg hurt, for being a child of the post war years he hadn't had enough calcium and his bones were brittle, even though he used to stride all round the country with a rucksack on his back.

The drunken comrades, supposing that the problem with his leg was that it was dislocated, and knowing nothing about calcium, roared with laughter and gave Sergei P.'s leg a jerk – with the aim of putting the joint back in the socket, which made the student lose consciousness momentarily, so they carried him over to a camp-bed, and put him on a bearskin there, which had been brought back from his distant expeditions.

When he came to, he demanded rum, vodka, wine and cognac in bed, and when they brought him all that he asked for, he cheered up again.

And the guests cheered up too. They started dancing the *Cracovienne* again, the *Tsyganochka*, the dance where you take it in turns to call each other in, rock and roll, boogie-woogie, and the twist, with the result that when the ambulance arrived and discovered dancing going on, the crew took against the patient from the word go and inquired angrily where he was.

Roaring with laughter, the guests pointed at the prostrate Sergei P. Sergei P. offered the ambulancemen a drink. The ambulancemen declined coarsely and angrily, and suggested to Sergei P.that if he wanted to be treated, he could make his own way down to the ambulance.

The guests linked arms and tried to carry Sergei P. down, since the lift wasn't working, but he tore himself away, and with a cry of "Fascists!", he went down the stairs by himself, hopping on his good leg.

Of course at the hospital they put his leg in plaster, having ascertained with the help of an X-ray that there was a fracture, but the case notes stated that he was "brought in in a state of extreme alcoholic intoxication", which did not at all correspond with reality, since he was in his usual, and not an extreme, state of alcoholic intoxication, and this was proved by the fact that on his return from the hospital in a taxi he carried on drinking until morning, and after dinner had a hair of the dog that bit him, lying in the marital bed and quizzically examining his brand new plastercast.

Then, always full of beans, his cross-eyed beautiful wife, Galka proposed a crackpot plan to her husband. That they get their skis, take a taxi to Izmailovsky Park, and that there he fall over on a snow-covered path, having taken his plaster off beforehand, and she would call the ambulance once again, and they'd put him in plaster again, and make out a new set of case notes, in which this time there would be no mention of the student's alcoholic state.

And that's what they did. I don't know if their plan was entirely successful, or only partially successful, but Sergei P. hasn't graduated from the institute to this very day, even though about 15 years have passed since then. Sergei P. has had, has and will continue to have many misfortunes in life. He got divorced from Galka, and then through match-making married, for her money and connections, some awful bulging-eyed bitch, who had two children by him, and then fiddled him out of the apartment which he had received, when, as a result of major renovation work to no.6 Suvorovsky Boulevard, he was rehoused in Yasenevo, being offered a one-room apartment with all mod. cons. and a huge balcony from which one had a marvellous view of the surrounding woods, the former estate of the Trubetskois and the Church of Anna in Uzkoe.

She fiddled him and kicked him out of home, so no one knows where he lives now. He was up in court twice, but got acquitted both times. He was beaten half to death in the city of Baikalsk in Irkutsk region and in the town of Rakvere in the Estonian SSR. He worked as the head of a geological team and once lost his briefcase containing all his business papers, cheque book, and the official stamp. "It was all a result of my going to a school for idiots," Sergei P., my comrade from the institute, who never obtained his engineer's-geologist's degree, always asserted.

Yet I obtained my degree, but what's the use of it? I don't work as a geologist, I don't know what I do, although I live, one has to admit, not badly, and I'm extremely satisfied with my life. Frankly, one might say, I salute life, just like that cat which a female acquaintance of mine, the literary critic Sh. brought home from the rubbish dump and gave a saucer of milk to. And this cat, once lost on a rubbish dump, as it drank its milk, kept saluting with its paw, just as, apparently, its former owners had taught it ... It is extremely satisfied with its life, all the more so now that with every day that passes life becomes more intelligent and interesting, as A.P.Chekhov predicted in his works.

And to your somewhat uncouth question, Ferfichkin, as to whether I have REALLY gone off my head, in interrupting my already obliterated narrative for the sake of a detailed description of the drunken escapades of one worthless Sergei P., who in formal terms has no right to have any relationship to my narrative, and especially to that part of it which describes D.A.Prigov and myself conducting our funereal wanderings, I will give you an honest answer: taking advantage of my official position as author, I am giving Sergei Dormidontovich Pauker a place in history through the old-boy network. Because he, and I, and my darling wife Sveta, and Prigov, and you, Ferfichkin, and many people, all the others – we're all going to die some time and our bodies will turn into dust, but paper is eternal, even when it is unpublished, even when it is burnt in a fireplace, like the second volume of Gogol's brilliant work, or burnt in a simple stove, like individual simple works by various authors at various times. And I did it. It was by virtue of the old-boy network also because I became deeply indebted to my institute comrade Pauker. He was always very kind to me, while I was always very rude to him. ("Even in the forests and swamps and far away, the OLD-BOY NETWORK rules OK ..." A.Pushkin – I recently read these serious lines etched on the dungeon walls of the Pushkinskaya metropolitan station). Rude, for I could not tolerate his loutishness, his over familiarity and vicious drunkenness, which made me call him a bastard more than once. Yet in actual fact, he was, apparently, as the humanists of the '60s considered, a kind man, somehow vulnerable in places, behind the affected cynicism there lurked a deeply vulnerable soul, and WE OURSELVES WERE TO BLAME FOR A GREAT DEAL. Do you love this phrase, Ferfichkin? ... It's not out of the question, for example, that the rum which we had drunk gave birth in his mind to the devilish plan to divorce his wife Galka, for to start with he wasn't a scoundrel or slob, I saw photographs of him as a child. And also, he was always lending me money. And also, I lived at his place, communal apartment no. 5 with its view onto the aforementioned Arbat courtyard. To be more precise, I didn't "live" there, I "made use of" the room. I was registered for residence in the town of D. in the Moscow region, which is on the Moscow-Volga Canal, and he went off on an expedition to the Urals and left me the keys. At that time I used to go assiduously to the place which I and my litbro E. got chucked out of in May 1979, and sometimes I had to stay the night in Moscow after various cultural measures were undertaken and after readings of my own works in various spots around Moscow. And after reading my own works in various spots around Moscow I had nowhere to sleep, so I used to spend the night at apartment no.5 block no.6, Suvorovsky Boulevard ...

So you understand yourself, Ferfichkin, here I am, hard at it, and paying my debts. IN GRATITUDE FOR THE PARTICIPATION IN MY FATE OF MY COMRADE FROM THE INSTITUTE, SERGEI P., by means of the old-boy network I include him in my epistles to you, even though I admit that his name is, apparently, unfit for your refined ears. Forgive me, Ferfichkin!

After major renovation work to block no.6 had been carried out, apartment no.5 became the legal and contracts department of VAAP, where a remarkable official, the grandson of a famed Soviet military leader, who had commanded the cavalry, helped me to wrest 500 roubles from a book publisher in the city of K., situated on the great Siberian river E., when this publisher, in flagrant violation of the legal-contractual regulations that existed in our country, refused to publish my modest compositions, but that's another story altogether, and I haven't got time to go in to it now, Ferfichkin, especially as there is nothing out of the ordinary in it ... It is the story, pure and simple, of how justice triumphed, which is as it should be always and everywhere ... I haven't got time, I haven't got time ...

25 December 1982

Because now, having received 500 roubles of my own money, I'm going to praise everything. It's great living in this world! You can compose something. You can take up your pen and paper and dash something off – no one will object. And parallel with the process of "dashing" something off, you can watch Kalman's operetta *The Princess of the Circus* on the television – who's going to say anything against that? Maybe Mr X. will be singing? He was a personage who acquired extraordinary popularity in the

'60s through his rendition of his plaintive existential song "I am weary of warming myself at another's fire", such was his popularity that the writers and poets of those years even put this "mister" in their short stories, novels and poems. And the readers demanded no explanations as to who Mr X. was, understanding that he was a perfectly respectable mister. Even my friend Eduard Prusonov, now holder of the Lenin Komsomol prize, once wrote a story in which either an astronaut or somebody else important, got drunk in a pub, sang this very song, and then BETRAYED a chance drinking companion, undoubtedly the *alter ego* of the author, yet there is nothing at all surprising in this, for the theme of BETRAYAL is the key to understanding the literature of the '60s. So now then, this very same Mr X. has started singing, playing the part of a snub-nosed actor unknown to me, whose fame will last but a day, for there is no majesty in him, and none of that all-powerful monumentalism such as were to be found in Georg Ots, I maintain, as I am momentarily reincarnated as an old man of the '60s. After his musical singing Mr X. overheard people talking about him on the other side of the wall, and he argued with some unkempt officers who tried to make him take his mask off . . . And now he's singing his heart out with N.Belokhvostikova, who is, it turns out, some COUNTESS PALINSKAYA. No, I don't like all this MODERNISM! All sorts of insertions and flashbacks! What do I need insertions for, what do I need flashbacks for! There was a time when Mr X.'s part was taken by the late G.Ots, while the late G.Yaron played Pelikan! . . . I remember, I remember everything – I remember hearing the radio show . . . in the city of K., on the river E., at the dawn of the scientific-technical revolution I heard . . . And there was another marvellous performer – the actress Bogdanova-Chesnokova from Leningrad . . . Yes, I remember now as well, she was sort of funny . . . Everything was much more

113

funny in the old days. Today it's not like that and it's not right. And then, what is all this rambling?

> Ah, those girls, the tights they wore,
> Really made our hearts so sore.

That's dishonest! There used to be some sort of other words, if I remember correctly ...

> Into the arena I come and stare,
> Smiling at the people there.

Etcetera. However, I could be mistaken, no one is insured against mistakes. The time is 20 hours and 45 minutes. In 15 minutes "Vremya" will be on. I have a hunch, a hunch, that it will be much more interesting than that so-called "princess".

> I'm a circus performer, a clown, OK?
> Let the bigwigs call me that, I say ...

So then! Although, of course, I don't want to offend anyone, and if anyone has lost his temper with me, then I sincerely beg his pardon, like at Easter: perhaps it's me who has been outstripped by life, and Mr X. and art have taken such enormous strides forward that I, poor little blind wretch that I am, can't distinguish between them at this distance. Or maybe it's the other way round. Perhaps it's I and my "brothers in literature" who are now so distant that we can no longer be seen with the naked eye, but only with the aid of some kind of optical device. I don't know ... For myself, let me say, just to make it crystal clear, that I'm not to blame personally, for, probably, through my forebears on my father's side, I am, indeed, a congenital savage of folklore:

114

what I see – I sing about, in accordance with the formula much in vogue. And Mr X. has suddenly turned out to be a PREENCE on television. Ugh, rubbish! . . . why do we have such rubbish! . . .

However, in apartment no. 5 block no. 6 Suvorovsky Boulevard there is now deployed the legal and contracts department of VAAP, a nationwide agency for the protection of copyright and it was there that I brought my DENUNCIATION, entrusting it to that remarkable official, the young grandson of a famed Soviet military leader, whose surname I cannot, naturally, disclose here. The young grandson, sitting on a chair, once part of the furnishings of former apartment 5, wearing a velveteen jacket and dark glasses, was delighted to take the DENUNCIATION and immediately set things in motion, for his sharp mind discerned right away in the documents the undoubted rightness of my case and the well-attested offence. By which means, beaming with delight, I soon received at the Moscow post office my hard-earned 500 roubles, while my humble works have not been printed to this day in the city of K. due to circumstances which are nobody's fault. I'm not complaining: life is life, and circumstances which are nobody's fault are circumstances which are nobody's fault, but you give me my cash and let's hear no more about it! . . . It's not nice hanging on to other people's cash, and taking advantage of the fact that the author has had an argument with someone over circumstances which are nobody's fault, and the grandson of the military leader, the famed former commander of the 1st and 2nd cavalries, after whom a geographical point in the Kalmyk ASSR has been named, justly pointed out to the publishing firm the error of its ways, which means that – order, the law, good business practice do REALLY exist, as they have only just been saying on the television. And they have also said on the television that in accordance with the wishes of

Muscovite workers they would now strengthen discipline everywhere and combat slacking. Good for you, Muscovite workers, I say of the Muscovite workers. Whereas of myself I say, without any false modesty, that in this regard I find myself ahead of progress. Later on somewhere I may possibly decode the simple meaning of this sentence, or possibly I won't. All right, I'll decode it here and now: sometimes it seems to me that this – that is, the struggle against chaos and lack of discipline – is exactly what I have been occupied with all my life, suffering one defeat after another and retreating from positions that have been prepared in advance.

Well then, let's continue after this pause, praying to God and tearing myself away from the television, on which they have just shown a couple of academicians being awarded the Order of Lenin, followed promptly by some shots of the very beautiful city of Erevan. And now they're going on about some Russian being fitted with an artificial heart, the operation being performed by Vladimir Spiridonovich Gigauri, in response, apparently, to an American heart, which has recently been given to some American. Vladimir Spiridonovich tells the Americans he congratulates them on their artificial heart, but that our scientists have a different approach to the problem, because our man has to be more mobile, less connected to his source of nourishment. Also someone by the name of Vadik Repin has come first in the Wieniawski competition in Lublin . . . Lyublino . . . And now N.Ozerov will bring the viewers up to date with the sports news, and some spritely little whippersnapper in a white jacket zealously recounts how he "shared the silver" with someone. No, it's still great living in this world, it's great! (Spit, spit, spit over the left shoulder!) And I really will buy that second-hand Zaporozhets, after all, it's not just idle talk when people say that second-hand Zaporozhets cars have got awfully cheap these days because of over-production and the rise in the general standard of living of the people. So I'll save up my money and buy one. I'll pass my driving test and sit at the wheel. I've already studied the common herd enough thank you very much, I got one of my buttons torn off again on the bus yesterday, so why shouldn't I now buy a car and drive round the streets of Moscow like some Mr X. or other?

Well, look, I've gone chattering on again. And off the point again. This is bad ... It'sss ba-a-ad ... I'm ashamed once again and I'm in despair once again. "this is not the time to chatter, it's not the time to let the ink run so that the contours get almost completely washed out," I'll whisper to myself before immediately continuing once more the description of my FUNEREAL WANDERINGS with Dmitry Alexandrovich though the streets of lamenting evening Moscow.

You'll recall, I left myself and my companion on Suvorovsky Boulevard by the House of Journalists, where directly opposite, across the motorway Gogol sits in a courtyard, downcast and cast iron (sculptor N.A.Andreev). We wander on. We talk about ... And we see – the air has grown dark, the sorrowful lamps have been lit. Ah, everything here, on Suvorovsky, formerly Nikitsky, Boulevard, strikes a chord in my heart! In 1964, being a student, I took part in the workers' First of May demonstration, and our column formed up here at exactly this point, on Suvorovsky Boulevard, near the House of Journalists. I carried a portrait of N.S.Khrushchev, who retired that very autumn for reasons of health. Then, in 1964, we moved along Herzen Street across Manezhnaya, now 50 Years of October, Square. I saw the government. The police spoke through megaphones. At the end of Red Square, right by the river, immediately behind St Basil's Cathedral, stood a huge mobile green-coloured toilet, that people were going in and out of, and if you consider, Ferfichkin, that this detail of everyday life is out of place here and that they'll put me inside for it, then I will part with it without a qualm, even though I consider that this detail is POSITIVE, emphasizing concern for people. There wasn't any toilet. The police were talking through megaphones. Immediately behind St Basil's Cathedral (the Pokrovsky Cathedral) there was the river, and the chimneys of the P.G.Smidovich Moscow power station no.1 belched out their smoke. I carried a portrait of N.S.Khrushchev.

Another memory. If you go along Suvorovsky Boulevard up to the Nikita Gates and stand with your back to the Film Archive Cinema, where according to the memorial plaque N.P.Ogaryov spent his childhood years, then on the right-hand side you'll see the Church of the Great Ascension, where on 13 February 1831 the candle for Pushkin's wedding went out, and on the left-hand side, behind the grocery store there is a police station, whither in the spring of 1979, when famous literary events were in full swing, the 69-year-old poet L., native of Odessa, was summoned. To explain why he had smashed, with his fist, the glass table-top of some bureaucratic literary rat of the male sex. L. calmly recounted to the major that in the process of issuing to him, the suppliant, some insignificant certificate, the bureaucratic rat of the male sex insulted him by expressing, with occasional snorts, grunts and direct words, doubt as to whether he, L., had participated in the Great Patriotic War. Which made the poet L., who had fought right through the war and had campaign medals, feel insulted, outraged, and depressed, and, unable to restrain himself, he struck the thick glass on top of the table with his fist, accompanying this act with a stream of imprecations, for which he apologized to any ladies, women or girls who just chanced to be at the scene of the incident, if indeed they were present and if their pretty little ears just couldn't tolerate such soldierly coarseness of language. He, the 69 year-old poet L., apologized to the ladies, and was even prepared to put it in writing in their case, but there was no way he was going to apologize to that bureaucratic rat, that forty-five year old pup, who shouldn't dare, yes shouldn't dare, to humiliate a frontline soldier, a veteran of the Battle of Stalingrad, a man who had been shipwrecked in the Baltic and burnt on the Volga.

The police major was an elderly major. He heard the poet L. out attentively, attentively looked him up and down, and immediately understood that the person standing before him was, neither in theory nor in practice, capable of telling lies. And the major said that of course the poet L. should at his age practise a little more restraint, but that he, the major, understood everything and would not allow the rodent's statement to be taken any further. On the contrary, he would tear up this "statement" into tiny little pieces, because in our country no one is allowed to make a mockery of frontline fighters, and that he, the major, knew this perfectly well, since he too had been at the front, had taken the Austrian city of Vienna, had been awarded orders and medals, had been shell-shocked and wounded. The police major shook the poet L.'s hand, and the poet L. went out onto the porch. Everything was almost all right once again. I and my litbro E. and another poet L., but of the female sex, were waiting for the poet L. in a VAZ-2105 car. The fair lady L. was agitated, sighing deeply and smoking one cigarette after another. The poet L. stood for a moment on the porch of the police station, and then seated himself ceremoniously in the car, and we drove off in high spirits. Those were, as they say, "complicated" times, but we laughed a lot, cracked jokes and were much amused. According to the superstition, he who laughs a lot, is going to cry a lot later on.

119

This superstition is misleading. Sometimes you'll shed a few tears, of course, not without, but still ... none the less ... how can I put it more precisely? ... "Things are really bad, but thank God ..." – this, according to the words of the poet L., was how one famous Soviet marshal jokingly put it.

Dmitry Alexandrovich and I walked along Suvorovsky Boulevard and unhurriedly crossed Herzen Street onto

TVERSKOI BOULEVARD.

But before describing our funereal wanderings along Tverskoi Boulevard, let me just add this, since I've only just remembered: on Tverskoi Boulevard near the miserable little Luna café modern-day hippies now hold their meetings in a little garden – whether they're nazis, or pazis or punks, I don't know, and of course in this sense I've been outstripped by life, cut myself off from the people. Young people sit on park benches for hours, doing nothing, saying nothing, just smoking a lot of cheap cigarettes all the time, whose smoke has the specific aroma of dope. They wear broad-brimmed hats, torn leather coats, officers tunics with the epaulettes removed, and fine American jeans. These are personages of the male sex. The ladies, or the girls – I don't understand, I don't know which – have little veils over their eyes, but on the whole they do not dress as extravagantly as their male companions, though possibly, the pretentiousness of ladies' attire has become the norm these days, and so you don't notice it particularly any more. I don't know what these young people sitting on the benches on the Suvorovsky Boulevard are waiting for, and I confess, Ferfichkin, that this question no longer interests me, for truly it is said: "We are all of a different generation" (Evg. Popov "Billy Bones". Short story. Moscow. Manuscript. 1981.). So then! ...

And also, on this Suvorovsky Boulevard, in the entrance to block 6–b (architect E.L.Yokhelis), built in 1936 for the employees of the Ministry of the Great Northern Sea Passage, I stood rather often in the winter of 1963 warming myself by the hot radiator together with my plump girlfriend, a schoolgirl in the tenth grade, whose name I've forgotten now, but whose nickname I do remember – "the queen of the twist". She used to say that that was what they called her in school, she was lying most probably, that fat girl whose last name was Kozlova and whose first name was (now I remember) Elena. Elena Kozlova was very stupid, but, in her own way, very clever. She didn't give in to me, which made me suffer, and her too, naturally. We used to walk the streets to the point of stupefaction on those frosty evenings, the snow squeaking underfoot, because we had nowhere to go and lie down, and you couldn't get a bottle to drink because we didn't have any money, it was a long time before my student grant came. So we'd go into the entrance of the Ministry of the Great Northern Sea Passage building, and just stand there for hours, by the hot radiator . . . The people who lived there walked past us, giving us hostile looks. I had a hard youth! . . .

Oh, it was hard! . . . I had to go off to the Lenin Library and out of grief read Huxley, Dos Passos, Joyce, Zamyatin, Remizov, the early Ehrenburg, Panteleimon Romanov, Zoshchenko, Dobychin, Céline and other authors there, whose books today are given only to very learned people (the exception is Zoshchenko). I soon stopped meeting the fat girl, for the romantic period of my life was passing, and maturity was beginning, THE CAUSE, as one novel put it. And anyway, by that time I had found myself other girlfriends who were a bit more compliant, I won't conceal the fact from you, Ferfichkin . . .

Yes, THE CAUSE, as they say, I am, deep in thought, compelled to repeat, for once again I don't know why I keep remembering over and over again tiny, absurd details of I

121

don't know what ... I don't know ... But actually I don't know anything at all, I don't know, for example, why I'm writing to you, Ferfichkin, so that in the present concrete situation my ignorance is musical, chaos is temporarily suffering fiasco, and I, finding myself inside a glittering cloud of misty harmony, solemnly and sternly continue on my way to the accompaniment of the plaintive strains of the funereal trumpets.

26 December 1982

TVERSKOI BOULEVARD

was the first boulevard to appear in Moscow for the former Muscovite aristocracy to take their walks along. It was created in 19796 (that is the date that my hand suddenly wrote down, so I'm leaving it like that purely to authenticate the current moment) after the wall of the White City (architect S.Karin) was demolished. Tverskoi Boulevard originally had only white birch trees on it, but then they planted limes, maples, and elms, and opposite no.14 to this very day there is an oak, whose age, so the experts tell us, is well past 200 years.

To start with, of course, there is the new TASS building (block no.2/26, architect V.S.Egerev). There, in that building, there once worked a lady of my acquaintance, who looked like one of those child's inflatable rubber dolls, of the kind that they don't make any more ... God be with her, a peaceable woman has no place here at all. God be with TASS too – TASS shone bright and majestic, incidentally, TASS was always lit up in the evenings, the light from the ultra-contemporary TASS building with its horseshoe on the pediment, representing, so it was explained to me

122

recently, either electro-magnets or was it an electro something field? – I can't remember. Anyway, it symbolizes
communication in general, information in general, propa-
ganda in general by means of technology. So then! . . .

Now another quick excursion into the past. You can't help
but put in a good word for Romasha and the "Caucasus"
kebab house, which in the '60s of the C20th was situated on
Herzen (form. Bolshaya Nikitskaya) Street directly opposite
the present-day TASS building, right next door to the 'oldies'
Film Archive Cinema, so that some people even got them
mixed up, which I can affirm without hesitation, for I myself
have spent not a few fine drunken minutes at the generous
tables of this hospitable kebab house, eating at 10 o'clock in
the morning high quality *Kharcho* soup, wonderful kebabs,
delicious spicy sausages and other exquisite dishes, which
cannot be recalled here because of the struggle for economy
of space and time I have conducted on these pages. The food
was washed down with white wine. Everything was very,
very tasty, and relatively, of course, cheap. I know this,
though we were never the ones that paid. All of us – me,
B.E.Trosh, Vitasik the Deaf, Sanya Morozov the First, lived
at that time in the hostel on Studencheskaya Street, where
Romasha sometimes spent the night with us, when he came
back to Moscow from the gold-fields. In the evenings we
used to play "Journey from Petersburg to Leningrad",
taking a drink at each of the imaginary stops on the way,
which left us in a terrible state in the morning – we would
get up with the shakes, moaning, unable to look at one
another, let alone at the world at large.

We used to get on the metro, travel as far as the Arbat,
and then walk along a familiar path: Suvorovsky Boulevard,
the "oldies cinema", the "Caucasus". We walked along,
bad-tempered, not saying a word. We ordered our food
without conversing. But after the first glass, after the first

123

spoonful of hot, thick soup, our coarsened souls softened, and we would start talking to one another, recalling the intricacies of the previous day's journey, and giggling. By 11 o'clock in the morning we had become real human beings again, and would set off on our own routine affairs. Romasha, I would like to take this opportunity to thank you once again for your hospitality! We had practically no money, and you didn't begrudge us – you were earning money and you spent it, thank you, I'll never forget that. I can remember everything. I remember that sometimes some extremely famous people came into the "Caucasus" in the mornings. Once we even saw there ... no, I can't mention that resonant name, that surname which everyone knows ... I can't, no matter how much you ask, Ferfichkin. I just ca-an't! Because of circumstances which are no one's fault ...

And also, that same year, I bought myself some really horrible pink braces in GUM, since I'd heard that this was now the latest thing: wearing your braces so that people could see them. I bought these really horrible pink braces, took off my jacket, and seated myself in the kebab house, proud of my, as I was soon to realize, thoroughly indecent appearance, for these braces were, of course, NOT THE RIGHT ONES, and resembled like two peas in a pod what children used to call GARTERS for holding up stockings. I became agitated, as I threw occasional sideways glances at my fellow diners, the aforementioned Romasha, the poet N., now better known in his capacity as Secretary of the Moscow writers' organization, and an imposing young lady called Zina from the Red Guard publishing house, to whom the poet Andron Voskresensky wrote verses in the '60s, which I remember, because I remember everything, but which I am not going to cite here, because her surname figures in them, and that might be professionally damaging for her. But then again, why not? After all, you know . . . it's a snippet of that epoch . . . All the more so, as the verses speak particularly of peace and the young, yet there was nothing reprehensible in my acquaintance with Zina, and nothing to compromise this venerable matron, who to this very day works in the same publishing house, but has now attained the famous upper echelons on the steep social ladder, down which I tumbled head over heels. Here are those verses!

> I adore "apelsiny",
> In French it's "oranges".
> I can't live without Zina,
> Whose surname's Magranzh.

Zina Magranzh and Andron Voskresensky! Those were the days, weren't they, eh? Great! . . .

Dmitry Alexandrovich and I linked arms so as not to slip over on the ice, and we walked past the Drama Theatre on Malaya Bronnaya (chief director A.L.Dunaev, A.V.Efros is the ordinary director. There are 739 seats in the auditorium, all taken).

"Is it a long time since you last went to the Drama Theatre on Malaya Bronnaya, Dmitry Alexandrovich?" I asked D.A.Prigov.

"I've never been there, Evgeny Anatolyevich," replied D.A.Prigov.

"Then you've been to Poland, Dmitry Alexandrovich . . ."

"Czechoslovakia, Czechoslovakia, Evgeny Anatolyevich . . ."

Further, further, quicker, along the boulevard, ahead, to where the bright illuminations of Gorky Street are to hand, and the cast iron statue of A.S.Pushkin rises up like a crag. Yet the wanderers feel at their backs the cast iron back of

Kliment Arkadyevich Timiryazev, the brilliant popularizer of Darwinism and natural-scientific materialism, the author of works on the mechanism of photosynthesis, biological agronomy, and the methods of researching the physiology of plants. Heading a group of 107 professors he walked out of the university in 1911, protesting against the reactionary policies of the government in the sphere of higher education, but all the same he enjoyed well-deserved respect in the enlightened sections of Russian society. And later on, in Soviet society as well, which is why, in 1923, the sculptor S.D.Merkurov erected the aforementioned memorial.

Between Timiryazev and Pushkin . . . And also, by coincidence, the no.107 bus runs this way . . . It was pointless, incidentally, V.Mayakovsky saying to M.Bulgakov in 1927 the little word "TimERZYAev" (V.Kataev. *The Grass of Oblivion*. Moscow, Sovietsky Pisatel, 1969, p.307). You know, this has a certain little whiff of nihilism about it, a whiff of destruction and annihilation, and I don't like it these days. These days, you know, I'm all for togetherness, and possibly for the resurrection of one's fathers. These days, you know, I have perhaps decided . . . Well, how can I put it? . . . well . . . to put it crudely, perhaps I've decided to become a CONSERVATIVE, and perhaps I have already become one, and you, Ferfichkin, haven't even noticed, and perhaps I have always been one, and you, Ferfichkin, didn't notice . . . No one noticed . . . But perhaps I wasn't one, perhaps I haven't become one . . .

. . . Herzen was born in no.25, which is now the Gorky Literary Institute, God damn it, that institute, because it turned me down twice, in 1963 and in 1974, but I don't take any offence at them, we don't know who lost the most . . .

I'm jumping about all over the place like a flea, God damn me too, (spit three times, to be on the safe side, I'll make the sign of the cross) . . . What am I going on about the Literary

Institute for, when we haven't passed even the Moscow Arts Theatre yet. The new MAT. A citadel. Cautiously does Art peep out of its embrasures, incarcerated in a building costing many millions, timidly feasting its eyes on the denizens of the boulevards, people hurrying about their urgent business, or simple passers by, such as, for example, the above-mentioned dramatist Yu., whom I met here recently, and who, pointing his stick at the majestic building of that Temple of Art, uttered an obscenity which I daren't and do not wish to repeat, because I don't agree with it at all. For I have been in that citadel. At first I really liked it, but then I thought – what was it that I suddenly liked about it so much? So I don't know to this day whether I liked it there or not. Most probably I did, though life's an odd thing, and I often think that when an individual or a group of people achieve something, then it costs them, they immediately lose something important and primordially vital, for anything vital, once incarnated materially, rather quickly becomes moribund. There was nothing, but there was something. There is everything, but there is nothing. It is cold in these huge halls, where the smart set whoops it up and the waitress bangs open bottles of beer and mineral water . . . But would it be any better in a barn? Or in a Nissen hut? But how does one achieve harmony? How does one defeat chaos? I have no idea. Who does know? Does anyone know? Maybe someone does know, but he died a long time ago, and there's still no harmony, none at all. But there's still chaos, and plenty of it. And death, there's still plenty of that. However, there is also life as well, I admit, though it's an unequally matched line-up – life, death, harmony, chaos . . . The line-up is unequally matched, but is that my fault? . . .

And opposite the new MAT is the Pushkin Theatre, formerly Tairov's Kamerny Theatre, where, in 1950, poor Alexander Yakovlyevich sat on a bench on Tverskoi Boulevard, beholding with a dying tear in his eye the spiritual shell of his brainchild. He died that same year,1950. A.Ya. Tairov is buried in the Novodevichy cemetery. A sad or a happy fate? What is fate like? I don't know. What else is there to say about this life?

Of course, they didn't turn me down at the Literary Institute for nothing, I tell you straight. In the first place, I could have been a completely different person. Perhaps I could have been someone or other who might have done something or other . . . But in the second place, it was a bad business, for there was some kind of intrigue on the part of the Literary Institute regarding my rejection there, for example, one document disappeared, and another appeared in its place . . . Well, OK, I'm saying I won't take offence, I'd sooner save it for the future, so that we don't make similar mistakes again, which only cause harm, I won't take offence, only you mustn't get angry with me for not taking offence but just remembering. I remember the morose teacher B., in the yard of that same institute, writing a reference for me on the bonnet of his car to get me into the place from which I and my litbro E. were expelled because of circumstances that were no one's fault, and B. doesn't teach anywhere now, because he was asked not to. AUTUMN, ALL OUR POOR GARDEN SHEDS ITS LEAVES: Mr B., Ms L., Mr E . . . A., B., C., D., E . . . It's sad, but, ah, it's all such nonsense in the face of eternity or death, which, in actual fact, is what this is all about.

. . . There was no possiblility of getting on to Gorky Street. There was a thick cordon of plain clothes and uniformed police there, and even from a distance you could see the ribbon of people that wound its way round behind the "Russia" cinema swaying. Unfortunately I hadn't been to the Pushkin monument that day, so I don't have any right to say anything about it, and the same goes for the "Russia" cinema, the *Izvestiya* building, and the editorial offices of the *Moscow News*, which all surround that monument ...

The thick cordon of plain clothes and uniformed police was there all right, but we saw that the people were turning off somewhere without any qualms. We turned off too, following the people, and I think it was Sytinsky Lane, only I don't know in whose honour it was so named: I.D.Sytin, Russian publisher (1851–1934) or P.V.Sytin, a historian (1885–1968). I don't know and there's nowhere for me to find out, or rather, it's impossible, there's no time, there's no opportunity, I don't want to, I've got all mixed up, I'm in a hurry ... Circumstances are arising such that I am writing to you, Ferfichkin, totally submerged in the waters of the fast flowing Lethe, which have suddenly deposited me on the cosy bank of the Moscow-Volga Canal, and I'm now in the town of D. in the Moscow region, and it's summer and I've got a garden, that is, a vegetable garden, which I am cultivating, growing cabbages, parsley, radishes, carrots, dill and onions. And what kind of reference books can you have in a vegetable garden? There's nothing here apart from lilac, vegetable patches and dandelions. Their white down flies away at the least breeze, as will our whole life. So then, Ferfichkin ... You may now consider this miniscule excursus into idealistic wide open space concluded and merely a one-off, because I shall immediately return to the mourning Moscow of 1982 and I shall not abandon her again until the very end of my epistles to you.

... Sytinsky Lane, but we don't know in whose honour it was so named. Perhaps, it is purely and simply that in former times in this lane people ate until they were SATED? I can even remember that in the early '60s there was a jolly little building here with a kebab house in it called "Inguri" (?), and a pharmacy, a milk bar and tobacco kiosks. They blew this block up, and cleared the débris away with a bulldozer . . . There were houses there once, then there was an explosion, and then dust. The dust spread everywhere, and there on the huge end wall, that was erected afterwards, they stuck that huge ultra-modernistic clock, by which it is impossible to tell the time because its dial is incomprehensible to an ordinary person.That's electronics for you: some sort of little lines, flashing little dots . . . Where's the time? Where's the minutes? Where's the seconds? Incomprehensible . . . Look at that slogan hanging up next to it, you can understand that, but you can't understand how to tell the time by that "clock", which has been fixed there for decoration on that high blank wall in Sytinsky Lane, that was put there in exchange for the houses that were blown up, you just can't understand it, don't even try, don't waste any TIME on it, describe instead what there IS FOR THE TIME BEING . . .

. . . We turned off, following the people, and went round the back way through the yard of the "Harp" café. A famous artist lived there for a long time, the creator of a poster that is so famous, that I'm not going to describe this poster, because anyone would know the name of the artist right away, and that's no good to me at all. I've seen the master and I used to know his son Gavrik, who was at one time married to my friend's sister, a beautiful girl called Rimma, an intellectual girl. It was Gavrik who in 1968 gave me that sole, solitary volume of F.Kafka to have a read of, the preface to which, penned by B.Ryurikov, begins, as I recall, with the words: "Kafka, whose strained and morbid art . . ." (I'm not sure of the accuracy of the quotation.) This volume cost 50 roubles on the black market, but Gavrik, being classed as an artist as well, started doing a bit of trading himself in beautiful icons, calling them "boards", "eighters" and "niners", and now he doesn't live with the beautiful girl any more, he drives around in a Zhiguli, and his dad, not

130

long before his death, took to visiting the managers of large grocery stores, and telling them that he was the very man who had drawn "you remember that poster? . . ." For which, unobstructed, he would receive Finnish cervelat, black caviar, and the finest quality fish. Only for money, of course, only for money . . .

All right. It doesn't matter. Again that's not what . . .

We went under one more archway, and found ourselves on Gorky Street near the "Natasha" shop, where the cordon was, and promptly encountered that winding ribbon of people. The ribbon stretched from Mayakovsky Square to Pushkin Square along one of the better streets in Moscow, where in the evening it is as bright as day and the people's faces shine . . . Shuffling their feet, the people moved along slowly, hardly conversing with one another. Some had their heads hung down, others were carrying briefcases. Had they come from work? Had they been buying groceries? But it was Sunday . . . However, perhaps they did have some sort of groceries? . . . The absence of music and of traffic, the scraping of thousands of shoe soles . . . The ribbon wound its way, yes, that's it, behind the "Russia" cinema (an awkward turn of phrase, but it can't be helped) and there it turned into a tangled mass. There were too many of everybody there to make anything out, but the procession was clearly turning into Pushkin (form. Bolshaya Dmitrovka) Street, and heading for the Hall of Columns in the House of Unions.

Let me note here again: the police, their part-time voluntary helpers, and other stewards that evening were perfectly, outstandingly, absurdly polite. God preserve us, not a bit of pushing or rudeness. They say that one woman, on coming out of Pushkinskaya metro station, went up to a policeman, showed him her passport, and explained that she had come from Vladivostok, but wanted to pay her last respects too. "Certainly," said the policeman, having

131

examined her passport carefully and giving her a salute, "Just go along there, madam, as far as Mayakovsky Square, and when you get there, go and see the officer in charge of one of the columns, and you can go through with that column and pay your last respects . . ."

D.A.Prigov and I didn't know this. We mistakenly thought that only certain special people had the right to pay their last respects and walk about there, that was our mistake, but now we had no opportunity to correct it, for the time had passed, it had dissolved away into the black night of 14–15 November 1982.

A female acquaintance, who, being an expert on the theatre by calling and by profession, recounted how, on 14 November 1982, in the afternoon, she had wanted to deliver a manuscript that had been commissioned by the All-Russian Theatre Society, which has its offices on Gorky Street near the Eliseevsky Grocery Store no.1. On coming out of the metro station, she went up to a policeman, showed him her passport, and told him candidly that she could just as well take the manuscript in on any other day, it wasn't urgent. Having examined her passport carefully, the policeman saluted and allowed her through. She then candidly called into the ATS, handed in the manuscript and set off for the Eliseevsky no.1, which, in her own words, was fantastically empty, pretty much as it was in those days when, according to V.P.Kataev, V.Mayakovsky met O.Mandelstam in there, buying a small quantity of pink ham (V.Kataev. *The Grass of Oblivion*, Moscow, Sovietsky Pisatel, 1969). This acquaintance also, like Mandelstam, bought some ham, admired the interior of the main trading hall, with its double lighting and its rich stucco moulding, and then walked along a fantastically deserted Gorky Street, where she obtained in some thoroughly deserted shop an Indian terry bath towel. This acquaintance maintained that

132

there were, are and always would be goods to be had in our country, but that too great a number of our fellow-countrymen wanted, quite unjustifiably, to obtain these goods, and that was why at times there seemed to be never-ending shortages, pushing, shoving, swearing and people feeling alienated.

I disagree with her, but that's not relevant.

Dmitry Alexandrovich and I went up to a policeman, showed him our passports, and asked politely if we couldn't cross Pushkin Square, Strastnoi Boulevard and Petrovka Street to get into Kolobovsky Lane, where our studio was, because we were artists. One ought to note that we haven't got a studio here, never have had and never will, even though Dmitry Alexandrovich is a member of the Union of Artists of the USSR, though a studio there always was and is (whether it will be, I don't know, for they're pulling down this outhouse to build a new metro station) there in Kolobovsky Lane – the studio of our friend, the seventy-year-old handsome philanderer Nefed Nefedych, who again, not for the first time, is to be mentioned in the pages of these epistles.

Having examined our passports carefully, the policeman acknowledged us politely with the gesture duly prescribed in the police force, and suggested that we take the metro as far as Mayakovsky Square, from where, in his words, it would be possible to reach the required address, while avoiding the cordon. We followed this piece of advice promptly and with pleasure, rejoicing at the fact that no one apart from ourselves was going down into the metro, and that only the occasional person was coming up the escalator, and he was immediately being asked for his papers. We took the metro to Mayakovskaya, and came out unobstructed almost directly opposite the offices of the journal *Youth*, where there is a green luminous depiction of a girl, holding

133

a twig in her teeth. The subdued noise of the people from Gorky Street again reached our ears, and again they weren't letting people through there, so we just turned right on to Sadovaya (see sketch map above), and got as far as the first side turning. I can't remember the name of it, but I know that there is the "Soviet Composer" publishers on the corner, and there's a shop that sells records, sheet music, and everything else that can only have anything to do with Soviet composers.

Sadovaya was lively and, by virtue of this, somehow seemed outside the area of mourning. Passing cars drove off and disappeared into the bright underpass, pedestrians hurrying by wore their normal, workaday expressions. This was bad! We turned into the dark lane (Vorotnikovsky, that's what it's called, I remember now!) and set off practically parallel to Gorky Street.

And somehow or other, let's see (yes, we went through a connecting courtyard, under an archway, and through a gate), and let's see, there we were on Chekhov (form. Malaya Dmitrovka) Street, but the house of A.P.Chekhov himself, in which he lived from 1890–1892 and wrote the book *The Island of Sakhalin*, stayed on our left, while we went to the right, towards the place where, as before, the human stew seethed and stirred uneasily.

We went past something else, I don't remember what. We turned into a lane, I don't remember which, there's some embassy there still, and also some sort of factory, but what it is, I don't remember ... There's a lane running past the rear garden of the Hermitage, while inside the garden of the Hermitage is the Theatre of Miniatures, and in the Theatre of Miniatures works a friend of mine, and in this theatre I would very much like to have some play of mine staged, but I haven't got a sodding hope. I would also like to work in the Theatre of Miniatures, if it were different, but I haven't got a sodding hope of working there, no sodding hope of it being any different, only I don't feel offended. I delight in the free composition of these absurd pages, and I need nothing else for the current segment of time elapsing in them. In actual fact we have gone too far ahead. At first they were shooting us in the back, some were killed outright, others only wounded, others had bullets whistling past them. But now we've gone too far ahead, and we can't be seen or heard. We've hidden beyond the horizon, gentlemen and comrades. We are everywhere and nowhere. We have moved into a different dimension, and we simply aren't here. Farewell! Sometimes our troubled visage, belonging to no one, will suddenly be woven out of the air of real space and realistic time, but in general all is calm, all is calm, gentlemen and comrades. All is calm, for we are not, are not here. We weren't, we aren't, we won't be. We were, we are, we will be, keep calm!

The Hermitage Garden, the Hermitage Garden ... oh, Garden, Garden, at the dawn of the '60s I used to spend summer evenings here, in Karetny Row no.4, where on the 26th May 1896 the first cinematographic film was shown in Moscow, where Stanislavsky and Nemirovich-Danchenko put on performances from 1898–1901, one of which (of the performances) was, if I'm not mistaken, the famous *Coachman Genshel*, and if I am mistaken – excuse me, but you were the ones who turned me down for the Literary Institute; V.I.Ulyanov-Lenin paid a visit in 1900; oh, Garden, Garden, where in my student days there still existed wind music, and there were large mirrored globes on the paths sprinkled with red sand, the Garden where beneath those mirrored globes we drank tea from a huge, fat samovar, the Hermitage Garden, where even to this day there towers a huge brick shell, the gloomy housing for some future theatre, built absolutely at the wrong time, so people main-

135

tain, by the lessee Ya.V.Shchukin at the end of the First World War. Where is that Ya.V.Shchukin? Where is all this? I may be pushing myself forward a bit, but I'm still going to say timidly, shedding a few tears – oh, come on pals, couldn't you find just a tiny-weany bit of room for one of my plays in this non-existent theatre. I'm a quiet man. I'm a modest man. I'm really nothing. Don't you know? I don't know either. But who does know? Doesn't anybody know? All right then. We're off again, that is, not off on a journey, it was just Dmitry Alexandrovich and I walking closer towards the scene of an historical event.

So why am I going on and on about me all the time? Shouldn't I perhaps describe my companion? No, I don't think so. Such are the times we live in that if you describe a person, and say what you know about him, he'll up and take offence, or worse still it will GENUINELY harm him. No, it's better that I don't start describing D.A.Prigov, let him describe himself, he's so red hot at it. Or should I describe him anyway, eh? Perhaps I'll do it like this. I'll meet him in a few days and ask him: "Dmitry Alexandrovich, do you mind if I describe you in context?" If he says I may, then I'll describe him, but if he says I mustn't, then I won't describe him, let him describe himself then, and let him take offence at himself, if it GENUINELY harms him, but I won't describe him, why should I? but well, maybe I will describe him, after all, I have free will as well, you know, am I any worse than the next man or something? I'll up and describe D.A.Prigov. A writer has the right to describe whomsoever he wants. If I want to, I'll describe him, I don't have to do what anyone says. He said to me himself recently, and said it quite right too: "You're correct in thinking, Evgeny Anatolyevich, that you can't hide anything from the world at large, which is why you shouldn't try to hide anything from the world at large – only then will the world be good or indifferent towards you. And if you try to hide anything from the world, then out of curiosity the world will poke its nose in your burrow, and its nose is out of all proportion to your dimensions, and the world's nose will destroy your burrow and leave you a cripple." This is what Prigov said, or maybe it was me who said it to him, I can't remember now, or maybe it was someone else who said it or wrote it, but I thought it was Prigov – there are a lot of people about, and they're all talking and talking, and all writing and writing . . . What for?

Ooh, what with all this verbiage I forgot to tell you something of historical importance about the monument to V.Mayakovsky, by the sculptor A.P.Kibalnikov, erected in 1958, and about the "Peking" Hotel, opened in 1956 (archiect D.N.Chechulin, 15 storeys, 209 rooms, accommodates 343), against the background of which this monument looks splendid. Yet what can I say about these two objects, when, in the first place, on that particular evening I didn't walk past them, but only saw them in the distance and paid not the slightest bit of attention neither to the "Peking", nor to the "agitator and rebel-rouser", and in the second place, when Mayakovsky Square was seething at the end of the '50s and the very early '60s, that is, when creative young people were reading their various works by the "Mayak", as we can see in the popular film *Moscow Doesn't Believe Tears*, I was not yet to be found in this stern city, I was still modestly studying in schools no. 1, no. 10 and no. 20 in the Siberian city of K., and when I arrived in the capital and went to the Mayakovsky monument, then it was already all over. Though, possibly, not quite all over, but at that time I didn't know it, since I was moving in different circles. There was even a group of YSOGists, for example, which performed in our institute, members of a poetic association with an abbreviated name which could be sort of decoded as: Youngest Society of Geniuses. They performed from the platform, they had permission from the institute's management. And I even met one of them in 1964 in the apartment of someone I knew, the poet T., on the one hand also a genius, but no longer young, and on the other, the author of an official song about the cavalry. At that time this T. was always intending to write a play about Christ, he was always saying that he would sit down, right away, there and then, at his table and would write a real play ... yes-yes, don't be surprised, about Christ ... Rumour has it that these days he has settled down somewhere in the Asiatic North, works in television, has bought a motor-boat and a LUAZ car, and has published a little book of his own verses along with some translations of Soviet Asian poets. He is married for the fourth time, has children by all four wives, who have now probably all grown up, and are now all earning their keep, according to the law of the land.

Now the YSOGist E., whose name I don't know, but I'm certain it wasn't Leonid Gubanov, was, in 1964, lying dead drunk on a divan in the apartment of his comrade T., who was roughly 20 years older than him, and the YSOGist was wailing on that "Anastasia Ivanovna" (apparently, A.I. Tsvetaeva) had just given him a knitted waistcoat which had belonged to "Marina Ivanovna" (apparently, M.I. Tsvetaeva). And the then mother-in-law of the poet T. (his second), the dreadful woman, was trying to persuade her crazy son-in-law on no account to allow the young genius to stay the night, for, to judge by his appearance and what he was saying, he was perfectly capable of raping her twelve-year-old granddaughter, T.'s little girl. T. coarsely told "his mama" not to "talk rubbish". The mother-in-law took offence, she was a little old woman, not too steady on her feet, and she stormed off into another room. The genius E., so the story goes, has turned from an aesthete into a proletarian, and now works nights in a baker's stacking loaves of bread, but soon after 1964 the genius T., instead of writing a play about Christ, composed an official song about the cavalry, made a tidy packet, got awfully stuck up and bought himself Vietnamese mats, an Optima typewriter and right at the end of the '60s chased his wife with an axe when he was drunk. That was when I, by now an engineer, chanced to be in the capital, and we started drinking together, fell asleep on the afore-mentioned mats, having guzzled all the French cognac which his wife, much encouraged by the success of "the cavalry", had been saving for her visiting teacher of French – though no one went abroad in those days, the thought never entered your head. His wife was also very progressive, and when I told them that I was weighing up whether I ought to join the Komsomol (1963), they both gave me a studied look and only many years later admitted what they had thought of me at the time ... They were poor in those days, almost destitute, but their house was always open and hospitable.

But right at the end of the '60s, one hot summer morning, I stopped the poet T. running after his wife with an axe when he was drunk, and he and I went into a pub, where I (I admit it all, this is my confession!) promptly got as drunk as a pair of cockroaches and, standing alone on the tramlines on Lomonovsky Prospect, I bawled at passers-by that I was also a genius and a pupil of V.P.Kataev, from whom, up till now, I had received my first and only letter, in which the great master had condescendingly encouraged me in my initial attempts at prose ...

So regarding the Mayakovsky monument and the hotel "Peking" I have nothing of historical interest to relate, except for the fact that it was in this square that the Contemporary Theatre was situated, which at that time was harder to get into than the Theatre on the Taganka is now. Once, "as part of a package deal", I obtained a ticket for *The Appointment*, a stage production based on the play by the humanist A.Volodin, and I remember this production very well, because immediately afterwards I got robbed in Sadovo-Kudinskaya Street near the A.P.Chekhov museum, where he lived from 1886–1890. This is how it happened. I was walking along, engrossed in my own agitated thoughts on the contemporaneity of Soviet progressive art and its future, walking along, recalling the witty exchanges on stage and the explosive reactions of the audience to the stage "truth", when I suddenly noticed that I was ringed by some young people, who, at 9 o'clock on a summer's evening, right in the centre of Moscow, twisted my arms behind my back, dragged me through a gate, and playing gangsters, ordered me to face the wall and put my hands on the back of my head. They ran their hands over my pockets. Their frisking and patting movements suddenly became uncertain, and someone's voice boomed out: "Where's your money?" "I haven't got any. You should have asked me in the first place, and I would have told you right away I haven't got any." I replied cheekily, trembling in my boots. "Walk straight ahead and don't look back, you shit," the Voice said indistinctly. They turned me away from the wall, and I walked, and then ran, into Konyukovsky Lane, where a drinking friend of mine lived. He was drinking that very evening too. He, and his crowd, were always drinking, and playing cards. They all got very worked up, and grabbing empty bottles, forks and kitchen knives, they dashed across Vostanie (form. Kudrinskaya) Square in search of my assailants, with me directing operations. My assailants were not to be found, and we all went back to the communal flat in the two-storied wooden house, propped up by a log of wood, near the famous Vysotsky grocery store (arch. M.V.Posokhin and A.A.Midoyants, 1950–1954), from which in winter we stole empty boxes for the simple purpose of heating the stove, we went back to the communal flat and drank long and hard, eating black bread, potatoes and mayonnaise ... So then ... My friend was called Grisha Strukov. So then ... And in the mean time, my two heroes D.A.Prigov and I myself, Evgeny Anatolyevich, finally crossed Petrovka Street near PETROVKA-38, and there the police finally stopped us.

27 December 1982

Or, to be more precise, we stopped the police. We asked extremely politely how we could get into Kolobovsky Lane, because we were artists. We had a studio there. Extremely politely, they asked us to show our documents ...

I haven't yet described the editorial offices of a journal we went past. However, is it worth it? No, it's not ... What there was has long been forgotten ...

Yet I do remember that at the time, in 1976, I was seething, upset and indignant, saying it was quite unjust. I remember even intending to write a letter to the late editor P. telling him to pay some attention to these disgraceful goings on. Saying that 2 short stories, approved BY HIM PERSONALLY and which I had put the FINISHING TOUCHES to, were being returned to me without any apparent grounds, and this wasn't right and it wasn't just. And that YOU YOURSELF actually INVITED me TO WORK on the journal, which makes it all the more offensive, though one might ask, what difference did it make? ...

Oh, all right then ... that's enough whingeing, must get on with the business in hand ... I remember that then, in 1976, I came out into the street, sighed deeply – it was spring, and sticky little leaves dozed on the trees ... I sighed, stood there for a moment, and moved off to bustle about Moscow, into editorial offices and publishing houses ...

141

All right . . . That's enough . . . Business in hand, must get on with the business in hand, young man. Business. Get on with it. And no whingeing and moaning. So we will further proceed along our funereal

path. We stopped a patrol, and stamping our feet and arm in arm, like two old Moscow women, asked extremely politely if we couldn't go across Petrovka into Kolobovsky Lane, because we were artists and we had our studio there. Extremely politely, they asked us to show our documents. We showed them, by all means. "Please go along here, comrades. You can't turn right, go straight on, and turn left there through the connecting yard," they said to us, having examined our documents carefully and saluted.

We crossed brightly lit Petrovka Street. In the distance the swaying of the mirage continued, but only in the form of the cordon, not the crowds of people, for Petrovka itself was deserted. It wasn't on the route.

We went down Sredny Karetny Lane where to the right was the end elevation of the building known as PETROVKA-38, and to the left was a spiral-shaped two-storied garage built at the end of the '20s, and the Sverdlovsky district committee of the CPSU, we walked through those prohibited nooks and crannies, hymned by V.Vysotsky, turned off to the right at the "Food Orders Department" shop . . . And it turned out that all the time we were circling around the forbidding building of PETROVKA-38, which is always on the alert, and whose lights still burn even beyond midnight in its humourless windows. Now there's an interesting question, is there a rising crime wave in Moscow or not? Is it often that, and at what times do, people get murdered, mugged, raped, stripped, robbed etcetera . . . Judging by the dimensions of the building, yes there is a lot of criminality. Judging by the fact that the building's dimensions don't change, no there isn't. Ah, if only the urges and desires of all citizens without exception could be made to accord with the law, how marvellous life would be! And as for those patholo- gical personalities who think nothing of sticking a knife into a living body and sending a living soul up to the blue yonder – they ought to be reformed by means of special tablets, but not like in *A Clockwork Orange*, for that's the West and capitalism, but in our own way somehow, in a socialist manner. So that they themselves understand that KILLING IS BAD! One must not deprive a living being of life, for God has given this being life, and He will take it away when He needs to. (Perhaps He needs to at this very moment?) I don't know . . .

And there's something else. "Well, what about," the little boy Fedya asks, "What about cows and lambs and geese and chickens? Are you allowed to kill sheat-fish with a mallet? Are you allowed to cut pigs' throats?"

"Chop down a Christmas tree? Blow up a cliff face with dynamite? They do that, you know – stick the dynamite in, and then there's no cliff! . . ." he goes on.

Ah, my boy, ah, Fedya! I don't know, honestly! I don't know, but I believe: that if you smite dead a living human body, it will be worse for you when you blaze with eternal fire in fiery Gehenna. But you can't kill the spirit, no matter how you try. A spirit killed is a nonsense. The murder of a spirit increases the weight of the stone round the neck of the murderer, but the overall quantity of spirituality in this world cannot be diminished, no matter how you try. It's a basic law of reproduction . . .

. . . However, the fact is, the New Year is just around the corner, but I still can't get past the frontier of 14 November

143

1982! Perhaps I should decrease the volume of epistles? Break them off right now, at this very line, at this word, at this lett ...

Or keep my tongue in check, so that my stupidity doesn't seem so obvious. Otherwise, look at all this rubbish I've churned out ... spirit, murder, fiery Gehenna ... All this is what they call pseudo-profundity of thought, or shallow (flat) philosophy. Dreadful! – that's what I say.

29 December 1982

For in struggling to fulfil the plan, rushing the job and cooking the books, now at the end of the year I've tangibly lowered the quality of the goods produced without maintaining the quantity required. I've started spinning out some yarns that now have nothing to do with these epistles, and that's bad, because from a bird's eye view, the poverty, limpness and wretchedness of my epistles will be exposed by Ferfichkin. They're just the same thing over and over again, they've been going on and on and on, they're still going on and on and on. Historical houses, extra-historical people. Personae "non gratae", and if they've been "gratae", then only just, only a tiny bit ...

All right. For the last time I'm obliged to pull my socks up, and observing scrupulous precision, I'll bring our funereal wanderings to the logical conclusion of the epistles, of which you may be assured, Ferfichkin, sooner than you think, I'm telling you precisely, I've never yet lied to you once in my whole life.

We came out of the connecting courtyards into Kolobovsky Lane and decided to call a halt at Nefed Nefedych's, for the semi-subterranean premises of his studio, full of sculptures, were white and welcoming at the back of one of those dirty little yards in the afore-mentioned lane. Just two words for history's sake concerning Nefed Nefedych. Nefed Nefedych, a famous Muscovite, has a fascinating, and at the same time trivial, biography. He was born and grew up in Siberia, on the river E. which makes him my fellow-country-man and we're on friendly terms. At the end of the '30s he entered the Moscow Art Institute, and was then sentenced to 11 or 14 years during the period of mass repression, which acts were justly condemned at the XXth and XXIInd party congresses, so that he returned to Moscow only after 1956 and was able to finish his course at the institute.

In 1959, having obtained his diploma, he became a party member and got a well paid job on one of the Moscow journals, which he left at the start of 1969, almost having been deprived of his membership through circumstances that were no one's fault. But he soon took retirement – he was approaching that age – so as to get a pension, and they paid him a good pension, 120 roubles, which was the same as my salary. His time in the camps was also counted as a part of his working career, and that's only just and reasonable.

Once in retirement, Nefed Nefedych devoted himself entirely to artistic work, and because of that, again got into a lot of trouble. In particular he was forced to leave his wife, since she hindered him in his study of mankind, or more particularly in his study of womankind, her attitude running in complete and utter contradiction to the unrestrained ardour of his nature. And all sorts of other fortunes befell him, which ought not to be recalled on this solemn and funereal day. Not having a corner of living space of our own for a time, my wife and I lived in his studio, and once, also in November, the same time of the month as today, one charming November evening in 1980 . . . Well, all right then. It's water under the bridge. That's enough recollections.

This isn't the time for them, it isn't the place, we must move on, boldly wandering in space and time ... It's water under the bridge. I tell you frankly, basing myself on my own experience ...

The bell jangled, and the old man came to the door excitedly. Grey wisps of hair hung round the edges of his bald head, and his eyebrows were also just wisps of grey hair. He kept on and on that he didn't have any vodka, he didn't have any wine, ah, what a pity it was that he didn't have any wine, any wine, what a pity that we hadn't brought any vodka, any vodka, it would have been so, so appropriate ... And let me just remark that Nefed Nefedych was in no way an alcoholic or the heavy drinking type. Of course, he liked to have a drink, like everybody, but not to the extent of shouting: "Wine! Wine!" Anyway, he wasn't shouting. He just kept repeating simply and gloomily: "Wine, wine ..." – and you're sure to understand, Ferfichkin, that this was just a manifestation in him of spiritual agitation brought on by the solemnity and historicity of the moment. Nefed Nefedych is famous not for wine, but for his irrepressible *politesse*, which had not diminished over the years, rather the opposite. Nefed Nefedych always neatly pressed his trousers and as soon as twilight fell, headed for Strastnoi Boulevard to pick up the tarts there, some of whom were only too pleased to go to his semi-subterranean premises, full of sculptures, where they immediately started jumping and skipping about, talking about art. You're right, you're right, Nefed Nefedych, morality among young people today has really slumped!

And Dmitry Alexandrovich Prigov is completely teetotal. I emphasize this again, addressing myself to future cultural historians, who in studying my epistles to Ferfichkin, might be suddenly led to imagine for some reason, that Dmitry Alexandrovich was a boozer. That is not true. He never touched spirits, and only drank beer, like a German, but in extremely moderate quantities: a bottle, at most two, or if it was in cans, then only a few cans of Heineken. He loved the song "Over the Mountain Tops". That's Dmitry Alexandrovich for you! Remember this illustrious name, Ferfichkin. Perhaps we will yet serve under his command, perhaps he'll be our brigadeer, hee-hee-hee . . . Or foreman, just like my grandfather was when he was working on the building site for the Forestry Institute.

And so, right then, we called in on Nefed Nefedych, and talked a bit about . . . Nefed Nefedych, was extremely excited, and said that, of course . . . I replied that it wasn't out of the question. "Yes," said Dmitry Alexandrovich, adding his voice. "Wouldn't you like some tea?" asked Nefed Nefedych. "No," we said hastily. "It's time we were going." "Oh, sit here with me for a bit . . ." "No, no! It's time . . . It's time to go, otherwise we won't keep pace with History."

We said our goodbyes warmly and even somewhat jocularly to the old man, and went out into his dark, dingy little yard again. Out there, hemmed in by the stone houses, we were convinced that autumn had turned out warm and damp this year, but there was no quiet at all, no calm, but only the subdued noise of thousands of shoe soles, shuffling along, spreading out over the ground, and the burning street lamps made it bright outside, but there was no calm, no happpiness, there was nothing, apart from freedom.

The old man stood in the doorway. There was his silhouette in the vertical rectangle.

"Come again, come again!" he said, waving his hand, and my heart contracted. God . . .

Making our way through the yards, we came out on to Petrovsky Boulevard, and glancing to the right, at Petrovka, we again saw the cordon.

No, the whole wide world has conspired to act against me!
... Take today – no sooner have I picked up a clean sheet of
paper, so as to bring to its conclusion, as promised, at one
stroke, with one mighty burst of energy, the plot part of
these epistles, to recount actually how we got there and
what we saw when we did get there, when ... when my
water closet broke, and I was compelled to travel into TOWN
and see the onlyjustdescribedabove Nefed Nefedych,
whose bog was always breaking down, so he's got all sorts of
bog equipment, and in particular – a famous black "sucker".

I was mucking around with it for about two hours, I
reckon ... horrible sludge, the freezing cold water made my
hands ache ... Well, all right then. Down with naturalism! I
should have called out the plumber and given him a rouble,
but we haven't got a plumber, and he has no need at all of
my rouble, he's got more than enough of these roubles. He
needs something else, but what it is neither he nor I knows.
Perhaps he needs 10,000 roubles? I don't know, and that's
why I clean out my water closet myself. Look, I've cleaned it
out now, and having washed my hands superthoroughly,
disinfected them and softened them with some perfumed
cream I've borrowed from the wife, I now continue my life
in art ...

On Petrovka we saw the cordon again, and somewhat
down at heart, we turned left towards Trubnaya Square.
And our hearts fell, because in moving to the left we were
making something of a detour from the primary target of our
funereal wanderings – the Hall of Columns in the House of
Unions. However, it doesn't do to forget that the direct path
is not always the shortest and truest, the validity of which
axiom was promptly demonstrated.

We walked along Petrovsky Boulevard. I adore the boulevards of the Sadovaya ring road, which sprang up on the site of the demolished wall of the White City at the end of the 18th and beginning of the 19th centuries, and that includes Petrovsky, despite the fact that my favourite is, of course, Strastnoi. When I finished my course at the institute and was sent back to work in my native city of K., I used to have nostalgic dreams of the Strastnoi Boulevard, Strastnoi Boulevard in autumn, when the yellow leaves rustled underfoot and the bluish haze hung like a silver cobweb in the air . . .

"Unfortunately, it doesn't look like we're going to get any further, Evgeny Anatolyevich," said D.A.Prigov, his voice faltering.

"Unfortunately, that's right, Dmitry Alexandrovich, and it is not going to be our lot to become witnesses to the historical event," I replied, my voice faltering.

"No, we have ALREADY become witnesses to the historical event," retorted D.A.Prigov. "By reason of the fact that we have been walking the streets of evening Moscow, and using our heads while we've been doing it. These very WANDERINGS of ours, given WHERE we've been going to, are themselves historical . . ." We took to arguing, and when it at last became clear that we had nothing to argue about, and that we were saying roughly the same thing, some yellow walls and a blue cupola suddenly loomed in front of us in the semi-darkness . . . A church! We turned into a lane, and – oh wonders! – before us were the bright lights of Petrovka, not cordoned off, and we could go through there freely.

"But won't they probably stop us there, Dmitry Alexandrovich?" I suggested timidly.

"Then why didn't they stop us before, Evgeny Anatolyevich, if they're going to stop us now?" said D.A.Prigov, trying to make me see reason, and on seeing my cowardly hesitation, added restrainedly, his glasses flashing with sarcasm:

"After all, we're not doing anything bad or reprehensible. If they tell us that we haven't got the right to go any further, well then, we're not going to argue, are we? we'll just say we're sorry and come back. That's right, isn't it, Evgeny Anatolyevich?"

"That's right," I was forced to agree.

We came out onto an empty Petrovka.

Petrovka was empty.

I saw Petrovka empty at the time of the Olympic Games in 1980, when "out of towners" were not allowed into Moscow, and at that time we were living in Nefed Nefedych's studio, where later almost all my manuscripts were lost, but later still were almost all returned to me, exceptionally safe and sound, in beautiful files, I have seen Petrovka empty ...

But I have never seen Petrovka so empty, and I am not likely to see Petrovka so empty again.

There was no one there apart from ourselves and persons like us. Deserted Petrovka was quiet, and unobstructed, we delighted in the opulent architecture of her majestic buildings – the friezes, cornices, the Empire style, the modern style, etcetera. I say 'etc.' because I'm a dilettante, and I admire beauty solely in its pure form, without understanding its meaning, even though I would love to learn the styles and terms in architecture, since I'm trying to acquire some culture. I'm not one of Mao's Red Guardists, or a left-wing extremist, or a beatnik, or a punk – I'm just a simple man, and I want happiness for myself and my Homeland. I'll take things in order: first I'll buy a second-hand Zaporozhets, then I'll learn English, then I'll learn the whole of culture properly, it's high time I did ...

"Look at that, isn't it beautiful, Dmitry Alexandrovich!" I said, holding my breath.

"I can see, Evgeny Anatolyevich," responded D.A. Prigov, growing serious.

We took off our hats, because we suddenly felt hot, and it wasn't surprising: the autumn was exceptional that year, and winter had only arrived yesterday, that is 28 December. It was only yesterday that the snow settled, and more or less took hold. Up till then it had been nothing but fog and more fog, and rain. +4°C. Rain in December. Thaw. It seemed as if all of nature was weeping ... We put on our hats, because night had fallen and we could have unexpectedly caught a nasty cold – autumn warmth can be deceptive, you know. Autumn is autumn, Russia is Russia, we are us.

We passed Stoleshnikov Lane. Surprisingly, the "Red Poppy" café was open for some reason. We went in. I was planning on having a little nip of vodka, since in the foyer of the establishment, which was named after a popular ballet composed by R.M.Glière, they had recently opened the "Little Nip" bar so that people could get pissed with decorum, but the "Little Nip" was itself closed today, despite the café itself being in a state of openness. But I was planning on having a drink. What D.A.Prigov was planning on, I don't know. He was, after all, as I've already said, teetotal. He drank nothing but beer ...

We went into the café, sweeping the bamboo cane curtains aside. There were voluntary police helpers, policemen and the staff in white jackets sitting in the premises of the café. They all sat together and looked at us without a word.

"Have you got any tea?" we asked.

"No, we haven't," they replied, and without a word we left the "Red Poppy" café.

Empty Petrovka, deserted Petrovka ... Petrovsky Passage (Petrovka no.10, "Modern" style, architect Kalugin, bas-relief "The Worker" by scuplt. Manizer), the corner of Kuznetsky Bridge – the "Svetlana" store (former house of D.P.Tatishchev), house no. 3/6 – Ministry of the River Fleet, the new TsUM store, the old "Muir and Merrielees" one, and lastly, the Bolshoi Theatre ...

But what was this? There was the cordon in front of us again. And it was the same thing again and the same people at the cordon. That is – voluntary police helpers, the police, plain clothes men ... That is – we went up to the cordon and asked once again:

"Comrades, could you tell us, please, can we get through here to Sverdlov Square metro station?"

"Your documents?" we were asked in the politest of tones.

"Certainly," we replied and showed them.

AND WE WERE ALLOWED THROUGH!!!

That is, allowed through right into the centre! Well we really hadn't expected such success, that they would let us right into the heart of the capital! ... We didn't expect that! We walked on beneath the iron horses. There were still some members of the public there, you see, they had been heading for the theatre, but a small paper poster was now to be seen on the wall, announcing a change of programme. If I'm not mistaken, "Spartacus" had been changed for Vivaldi. No, more likely than not, I'm wrong. Should I ask Dmitry Alexandrovich? Well, he's probably forgotten by now. Everybody has forgotten everything ... All right, this minor historical detail will have to be left unclear ... Vivaldi ...

It is with shame, but still I must confess that we had told lies once or twice that day, reckoning that the end justified the means. Of course, we immediately forgot about going on the metro. We passed beneath P.K.Klodt's quadriga, pawed the ground a bit, like horses, and turned right, looking boldly and openly at the privates, NCOs, officers, senior policemen, and voluntary police helpers coming to meet us. We were expecting the question "Where are you going?", and were ready to answer: "We're going to see Teodor". That is, we wouldn't have said, of course, word for word: "We're going to see Teodor", we would have twisted it a bit, and said that "We're artists, and our studio is here" and so on, while once again pointing boldly at the high windows of the mansard in the two-storied house that looked out on to Theatre Square. But fortunately, no one asked us about anything, and freed from the necessity of having to tell lies, we really did go and see Teodor.

Teodor, an artist and good friend of D.A.Prigov, according to our calculations, most certainly had to be in his studio, for it was indeed in his windows that there were still lights burning there in the distance. We turned into Kopievsky Lane, packed with army lorries, and gasped: EVERYTHING was open before us, both a bit of Pushkin Street and a part of the House of Unions. We could distinctly hear genuine funereal music, and the winding ribbon of people shuffling, shuffling along, barely to be glimpsed behind the backs of the double police cordon.

I know Kopievsky Lane, how could I not know it! In the café on the corner of Pushkin Street, directly facing the Hall of Columns of the House of Unions, I once had lunch with P., the famous Soviet playwright (female gender). We were on friendly terms in those days, and as far as she could, she helped me with my literary affairs in the capital. The café was called "Sadko", and we went there in the spring of 1975 immediately after the 325th conference of young writers.

153

That year I had just forsaken Siberia, having got myself a splendid exchange of a three-roomed apartment in the centre of the city of K. for a quarter share in a house with stove heating in the city of D., which stands on the Moscow-Volga Canal. We talked about literature, and used the formal form of address, saying how difficult it was, almost impossible, to get anything published. P. got angry when she saw that I wanted to pay for our modest lunch, and she insisted that I accept her share of the cost.

There is also a "Little Nip" bar in Kopievsky Lane. I have been in this "Little Nip" too. Some drunken slob there, face all green, kept pestering me, telling me to have a shave, the woman in charge told him to keep quiet, and eyed my beard and tatty coat with respect. "That's not allowed ... you're not allowed to make a noise in here," she said for public consumption. "This is a respectable establishment, and respectable members of the public come here ..." I remember that pleased me a great deal at the time.

Dmitry Alexandrovich and I plunged into an archway. A soldier was smoking lazily in the yard. And another soldier was sitting in the cab of a lorry. And there was an aerial on the lorry.

We went up to Teodor's place. Teodor was genuinely astonished, and perhaps even delighted. Teodor is, after his own fashion, also a modernist, but at the same time, like D.A.Prigov, he is also a member of the Artists' Union of the USSR. "Nice work if you can get it," I mumble enviously into my beard, and my litbro E. supports me ... Teodor had a new picture on his easel, and you could guess that the customer, the head of some institution, factory, collective farm, or state farm, wouldn't pay for it, and the great artist would again be left without his money. It was written all over the picture and all over the couldn't-care-less face of the artist. Teodor's dog, named simply Beetle, was gnawing an old bone and growled menacingly whenever anyone of us went past. She was only pretending, because she too wouldn't have minded leading a run-of-the-mill life in the art world.

We started talking about ... Teodor said that his watch was broken, and he had turned on the transistor radio in the morning to get the time, since the windows in his studio were situated such that he couldn't see a street clock, only the theatre's stage-door entrance, which celebrities of the opera and ballet went in and out of. He had turned on the radio, heard the French words "la mort", and caught on immediately, always having been an innately bright lad. Teodor said that he hadn't seen any of his friends for two days now, and for two days now hadn't had anything proper to eat, since he was afraid of going outside the walls of the studio, and had only been taking the dog out to perform its bodily functions in the yard, where the soldier with the aerial sat bored. That he was afraid of not being able to get back into his studio, and then he would have to go home to live in his communal apartment, where he was registered for residence, but where he was to be found only extremely rarely because ... Teodor paused and filled his pipe with "Capstan". We asked him for something to smoke, explaining that we had run out of cigarettes, but he refused us, explaining that he never smoked cigarettes, whereupon D.A.Prigov, as were his rights as a good friend, gently but firmly suggested that he offer us some "Capstan" tobacco. Teodor fetched some pipes with long stems. The tobacco really did turn out to be "Capstan". We said: "Ooh-ooh ..." "We don't keep any old crap here," responded Teodor proudly.

... because Teodor's neighbour in the communal apartment sold milk straight from the barrel. He got up at 5

o'clock in the morning and went "to where he had his stall"
The barrel was delivered by 6 o'clock, and then he did a
roaring trade ... By 11 o'clock, when the wine stores
opened, his working day was completely over, seeing as the
barrel was completely empty. His neighbour gave back-
handers to anyone and everyone he needed to, and he
still had 40–50 roubles left over to call his own. He got
2–3 bottles of "Caucasus" port wine, each bottle 0.8 litres
in volume, and went off "home", that is back to the communal apartment he shared with Teodor. The home of
this fine milk vendor was an Aladdin's cave: There was
Finnish furniture, a colour television and video, a two-
hundred volume edition of treasures of world literature, a
"Madonna" dinner service, a "Rosenlew" refridgerator,
copies of *Queen Margot* and Maurice Druon novels, which
you can buy when you hand in waste paper you've col-
lected, but it's cold and freezing selling milk in the mornings,
and his neighbour put on padded trousers, a sleeveless
jacket, thermal underwear and a short fur coat. But back
home it was warm and life was merry. Back home he took
off his fur coat, his padded trousers, his sleeveless jacket,
and when he had a drink of "Caucasus" he walked about
the apartment in his underwear. The "Caucasus" worked
its magic, he stripped down to his vest and his black
sateen pants, and walked around the apartment again.
Sometimes he took all the rest off as well after the third
bottle. But he wasn't a nudist or exhibitionist, thank God.
He was a simple person. Twice he had chopped up the
furniture with a sabre, just like Oleg Tabakov, and he
had had an ampoule of antabuse surgically implanted,
but that hadn't made any difference – he got too much
money every day, and he had no idea what to do with the
money, and the port wine only cost about three roubles a
bottle.

Having said a hearty farewell to Teodor, we went out into the street. We looked at the soldier, the aerial, and then left the yard.

And then something happened to us which J.V.Stalin would most certainly have called "dizziness from success". We suddenly addressed a senior police officer with the most absurd words:

"You know, we are artists, we have our studio up there in the attic ... Couldn't we go out on to Pushkin Street ... Couldn't we just have a look ... That is, not go right out there, but if we could just go through your first cordon, we could just have a little look from behind the backs of the men in the second cordon ... like ... at Pushkin Street, at the Hall of Columns in the House of Unions ..."

And one must say that D.A.Prigov and I both looked exactly like real ARTISTS – beards sticking out, scarves flapping about, me smelling of wine ... And also it suddenly occurred to us that it was ARTISTS that they had taken a liking to that day, it wasn't for nothing that we had been let through everywhere. Or maybe it was that they liked EVERYBODY that day?

"No, you can't," said the officer, with a smile, and not understanding the meaning of his smile, we felt emboldened by it and started prattling on: "Pushkin Street, the attic ... artists ... a picture ..."

"No, you can't," repeated the policeman, again with a smile.

We walked away from him as if struck by thunder! For some new piece of knowledge had suddenly been revealed to us! If in fact he had really NOT BEEN ALLOWING US THROUGH, then he would have been answering us coarsely, weightily, tangibly, sharply, and precisely, but he DID NOT LET US THROUGH, AS THOUGH HE WERE LETTING US THROUGH. It seemed as if he was on the point of letting us through. But in actual fact, really, he didn't let us through, as though he were letting us through, that is, politely, almost condescendingly. Wonders will never cease!

There really were wonders to behold, even though it was plain to see from our example, that the common people were not to be molly-coddled. In the first place, Dmitry Alexandrovich and I had got through to places the devil knows where, places where, first and foremost, we really had no need to be, had no right to be, and where we weren't supposed to be, and in the second place, I want to ask once again – what kind of magic was it that the word ARTIST was exercising that day, why was it ARTISTS in particular that they had taken a liking to that day? And lightning once more illuminated the timid expanses of my brain – perhaps they loved EVERYONE that day? Perhaps, no matter what we were called that day – writers, painters, stage performers, metal workers, turret lathe operators, pharmacists, drilling workers, storemen, charwomen, or astronauts – they would have still let us all through, as long as the appropriate documents were in order?

I don't know.

We went out on to Theatre Square again. We were tired. It was high time we went home, back to Belyaevo, and Tyoply Stan, but D.A.Prigov and I had become, as it were, intoxicated, and we couldn't budge from the spot. We ought to have gone to the metro, but we skirted Sverdlov Square station again, and again went to the left towards the famous fountain opposite the quadriga, where in the '60s the Moscow "gays" used to gather in the evenings, and I, having arrived in Moscow in the summer of 1963, didn't know the special nature of this square, and having had supper in the Cool of the Day café, on the site of which there now stand a second-hand book shop and the statue of Ivan

Fyodorov, I sat down on a bench to have an evening smoke, while admiring the multi-coloured jets of water from the fountains, and I was awfully surprised when this nice old chap I was sitting next to evinced active concern for me. He set about inviting me to the town of Zhukovsky where he had a Volga car, and kept asking me if I had started going out with girls yet. I was awfully surprised! Well, not altogether, awfully. After a minute I realized what it was all about, and only out of the politeness that a provincial would show to an inhabitant of the capital, did I hear the chap out almost completely, before making a run for it, tearing his address up. The poor man kept shouting after me:

"Do come to Zhukovsky, I'll introduce you to some nice girls! ..."

Maybe he wasn't "gay" after all? Maybe it was all idle chatter – all this talk about the Theatre Square being the main stomping ground for homosexuals. Maybe he was a good, kind, straightforward person, and I just reminded him of his son, who was away serving in the army?

I don't know.

I do know that on 14 November 1982 at 23 hours and 11 minutes Dmitry Alexandrovich and I were attempting to peep round the corner of Sverdlov Square metro station so as to see absolutely EVERYTHING, but we soon abandoned these senseless endeavours, for to succeed one would have had to peep round two corners, which at present the human eye is incapable of doing. I feel that another sketch map is necessary.

THE MAIN SECTION OF DMITRY ALEXANDROVICH'S
AND EVGENY ANATOLYEVICH'S WANDERINGS

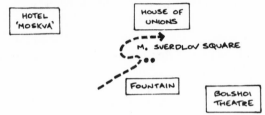

KEY:

- ━ ━   This is how you would have to peep to see
  absolutely EVERYTHING. It's impossible
- ●   Dmitry Alexandrovich
- ●   Evgeny Anatolyevich

30 December 1982

It's impossible! This morning I made up my mind once again
to finish it all off in one mighty, speedy burst of energy and,
at last, rid myself of the delusion – but no chance: I had
plenty of empty wine bottles and no money. I went off to the
shop, took a lot of bottles with me, on the off-chance, I live
dangerously. If not, not, I thought. If the shop's closed, I'll
dump the bottles out in the snow ... Though of course, it
would be a pity to dump 10 roubles (20 kopecks × 50 bottles)
in the snow. That was a relief: I could see even from a
distance that it was open, the queue wasn't too long, right, I
thought, I'll have the money back on the bottles in no
time ...

No chance! When I got up there I saw that the plywood
shutter on the window was closed, because they were
"loading bottles", and consequently, they were going by the
rule book. There was a notice on the wall saying that bottles
wouldn't be taken back while bottles were being loaded

and cases unloaded. There was the notice: "loading in progress". Tut-tut, dreadful state of affairs!

I was rooted to the spot, deep in thought – what should I do? But soon fortune smiled on me once again, for it became clear that the men, volunteers from the queue, had, off their own bat, almost finished loading the huge trailer. There, they'd finished now ... And they were all respectfully let in at the front of the queue, and we, the common folk, thanks to their selflessness, were able to hand in all the bottles we had, without a long wait ... Thank you, comrades! It took me altogether only 1 hour and 24 minutes to get 10 roubles. It was as if I had really EARNED 10 roubles ... It's a good life, it really is!

.. yet we were still dying for a smoke, because "Capstan" may be "Capstan", but we were used to a different kind of tobacco. Two young men with identical moustaches, but wearing different coats, were sitting on the bench there: one had a light overcoat, checked, while the other had a checked coat as well, but with a fur collar. We asked them for a smoke. They gave us a "Shipka", and eyed us with hesitant inquisitiveness. But when we sat down on the next bench along, they relaxed and went off, evidently taking us for two of their kind.

But we were our kind. Ordinary Soviet people. Comrades. We thoroughly enjoyed the smoke and looked around greedily. Another group of similar young men went by. They also eyed us with hesitant inquisitiveness. And they too went off to one side, and retreated into the background, reckoning that only people with a clear conscience and people who had an undoubted right to, could be puffing away on cigarettes in the very centre of the capital on a day like this and at this hour.

We kept our eyes peeled. A massive Icarus coach drew

up at the Bolshoi Theatre and a large number of coloured men got out. They lined up, and with an escort, filed round Sverdlov Square metro station (see sketch map no.2); a delegation from a fraternal country, we realized. The light from the street lamps in the city centre became diffused in the damp air. The quiet, muffled shuffling of thousands of feet formed a background. Three yellow-eyed Chaika cars turned sharply off Red Square. And other black cars kept arriving, arriving ... The following day we found out that anyone could have been sitting in those cars, any important personage, after all, on that particular day, on that particular evening, and it's not out of the question that at that particular hour, they all came to say their last farewells ...

Strange feelings: on the one hand we felt that we were involved in History, and were rejoicing in the distinct realization that none of our friends, acquaintances or relatives would be so close, on that day, that evening and that hour, to the geograhical epicentre of world history, but on the other hand, simultaneously, it was as if we were sitting in a Russian, Soviet kitchen in a one-room apartment, in which the one room housed a coffin containing the master of the house, and people kept calling in all the time ... And the women crying. And rain falling. And darkness outside the window. Tomorrow the day would arrive, there would be the funeral, frail men would carry the coffin, faltering so as not to bang it against the narrow walls and the bannisters ... I don't suppose there's anything criminal in these reflections of mine.

"I suggest to you, Evgeny Anatolyevich, that you remember all this for the rest of your life," said D.A.Prigov quietly.

"I should also like to suggest that to you, Dmitry Alexandrovich," I replied quietly.

"I agree, comrade!"

"And I agree, comrade! ..."

Sparrow Hills? Oh no, no, not that, not that . . .

After not speaking for a while, we decided to go home, for we had seen and heard all that we needed to.

The New Year is approaching and the plot part of my epistles is practically completed. There only remains to add that no one asked to see our documents any more. Unobstructed, we lingered by the famous fountain (arch. V.I.Dolganov), went down into the underpass, came out in the direction of the hotel bearing the name "Metropol" (that rang a bell), and cut across the square, pausing briefly near the luxurious cars, of the kind which likely as not belonged to the foreign guests in the hotel. From a distance we could see there, by the House of Unions, the corner of the House strangely changing in colour in the autumn night air, again we could see the various military men, the police, and their voluntary helpers, we went down into Revolution Square metro station, which was jam packed, and everyone we met stared at us with hesitant inquisitiveness, wondering whether we were ill, or mad, or drunk. But we were all right.

A last detail. When we went into the empty underpass, there was some thick-set major there, bored with being alone, reading a dog-eared book of some sort and leaning against some sort of iron box. When he saw us, he leapt up in fear, and made a clumsy attempt to hide the book behind his back. But when he realized that wigs we may have been, but not big ones, he stared at us with hesitant inquisitiveness, wondering whether we were ill, or mad, or drunk. But we were all right. In his demeanour the major reminded me of my friend the poet A.Leshchev, who in turn was the spitting image of Pierre Bezukhov, as described for the Russian reading public by Lev Tolstoy.

New Year, New Year! How much joy it usually brings people! Just today – as if to order, after all that sluggish autumn slush – there was a heavy snowfall, and at last, the temperature stabilized at -5°C, which is the essential and satisfactory condition for a classical Russian winter, as has been, is, and always will be, no matter what the circumstances are. The steam will pour out of your mouth, a beautiful woman, freezing cold, will wrap herself tighter in her warm furcoat, the bullfinch will perch on the branch, looking down with its round eyes, and some drunken bright spark will go for a swim in a hole in the ice at Epiphany, and footfalls will squeak on the snowy path, and there will be the expectation of spring, summer, autumn and a new winter . . . There will be everything, no matter what the circumstances. There will be everything, and nothing will give way. It cannot be that everything could give way all at once, disintegrate, be swept up by cosmic whirlwinds and disappear forever in space and time, and ultimate darkness descend, and hobgoblins come to rule for time immemorial where once there was life at play.

It remains to me to perform my last duty, that is – to acquaint you, Ferfichkin, with my utterly precise record of the progress of the procession. You see, on the next day, 15 November 1982, I didn't go out into the street, having reckoned in good time that I wouldn't be able to see anything anyway in the thick crowds. I went instead to see D.A.Prigov, who had suddenly emerged in a role quite unusual for him, that of proud owner of a colour television, around which we all seated ourselves. We were all drinking tea and eating honey, and watching the television.

Here is a detailed record of what I saw and heard, and don't you expect a single word more from me, Ferfichkin ...

Here is that record.

A gesture from the Master of Ceremonies – welcome. Top officials.

———

The widow, wearing a veil, rises to meet them. The New Leader gestures with his hand that she should stay seated. Kisses her.

———

M. phrase (Musical phrase? I can't remember now, yet altogether only a month has passed, and I made detailed notes). M. phrase is stern and sad ...

———

Yesterday evening there was a speech on TV by Comrade Ch., the editor. He said that the deceased had travelled hundreds of thousands of kilometres in the struggle for peace, and now he had a little less than 2 kms to go from the Hall of Columns in the House of Unions to the grave ... (What did he mean by this? It seems to me that a person is always mortal, and death will always overtake him, no matter how many good deeds he has done.)

———

14.X1.82. Requiem masses for "the late lamented" held in all the churches.

"He was decisive, bold, loyal in friendship, ready at any moment to come to the aid of a comrade."'
"He understood the best that is given (?) by human wisdom" (quotations. I don't remember from whom).

A monument in his native city. Prometheus. Promethean fire.

At 11 in the morning the clock on the Spassky Tower in the Kremlin chimes. A black bird flew past the clock.

At 11:15. The "Death March" from the *Eroica* grows louder.

"Nice drop of honey, this," he said, licking his lips.

Remembered a film. Who made the film? I haven't seen it.

No, not Fassbinder. Fassbinder's the same age as me. He's dead too.

11:20. Colonels carrying wreaths, generals and admirals carrying awards. Lots.

They're going along. Two (?) go off to one side. A military Master of Ceremonies ordered them to go to one side, even though, possibly, he's a 100 times lower than them in rank.

Military men lift the coffin. Requiem.

Top officials. They set the coffin on a gun carriage.

Where's the New Leader? Glimpse of the crowd. Sabres bared.

Car starts up, but I think it's outside. (By D.A.Prigov's house, not on the television.)

People looking, waving their arms. In the background.

Putting hats on, taking them off.

Military men and the music operating with precision. Civilians fussing.

11:30. We're off!

Top officials. Relatives in front, about 30 people. Wife, daughter, young man with a forelock. An officer.

What's this? Two catafalques? No, fault in TV transmission. Don't quite understand. Looks like the processsion is going perpendicular to Sverdlov Square metro station.

BBC. Strange-looking flag they've got. Sailors.

Commentator: "He was distressed by the abrupt change in the USA's policy."
    "His energy ... optimism ... with rare wit ..."

Photographers and film crews milling about.

They go up over the cobbles past the Historical Museum.
Huge trumpet from the wind orchestra fills the whole screen
of the colour television.

The journalist K. (he died shortly afterwards, on returning
from Afghanistan): "He leaves us a priceless legacy – a 15-
million-strong party . . . At any turn of events . . ."

Clattering. The head of the guard changed.

Wreaths against the Mausoleum.

Mausoleum.

Orchestra starts playing faster. Almost a waltz. Chopin's
"Funeral March"? Drum beating louder. I don't know
much about music.

Some of the wreaths on the left. They carry the portrait further.

Black birds wandering around on the cobbles on Red Square.

Close-up of his portrait behind glass in the Historical Museum.

Relatives' tread grows heavier. On the right a lady. She's the daughter.

They take hold of the coffin. Empty armoured troop carrier drives away quickly.

Top offficials. Carrying the coffin.

One of them fussing around the relatives.

Top officials. The tribune.

All packed up in time. Exactly 12:00. The New Leader addresses a mass meeting.

───────────

12:00. A sound. Coughing. A speech (see the newspapers for 16/X1. 1982).

───────────

Disposition on the Mausoleum from left to right (see the newspapers for 16/X1. 1982).

───────────

Colleagues of the deceased from other countries in the crowd by the Mausoleum.

───────────

Indira Gandhi.

───────────

"YOUR good work will remain ..." A military man speaks in the voice of the deceased (their voices are similar in timbre).

───────────

President of the Academy. He says "ContemporAneity".

───────────

A metal-driller, agent of the deceased at elections. An orator! Beautiful voice. Moscow Art Theatre modulations ...

Fellow-countryman from the south don't remember his name or job. Talks about the attention the deceased paid to fellow-countrymen.

Meeting over. One man makes to salute for some reason, but then quickly checks himself.

Carrying the coffin. Military men carrying it. Top officials in support. Two in front. The New Leader.

I take a peep out into the street. Everyone's in front of the television. Only children playing, and an old woman collecting empty bottles.

The carpet's rolled out. The top officials have gone away. Military men lifting the coffin on to a table covered with a crimsom table cloth.

The wife is helped forward. Wife and daughter.

Daughter kisses the deceased. The wife straightens his clothing.

The son. Balding, looks like the father.

They stand, not taking their eyes off HIM WHO ONCE WAS. Wife, daughter, son, relatives.

Panoramic view of Moscow.

Gesture from the New Leader.

Wreaths the length of the Kremlin Wall.

Touching pronouncement by D.A.Prigov stirs the soul of the patriot.

The soul of a patriot . . .

Of a patriot.

———————

They didn't show the farewell(?). And now they're getting
the coffin lid.

———————

Workers in black uniform in position. Grave-diggers?

———————

Women wearing black coats and black net veils. Carrying
black handbags. Relatives?

———————

Military man assisting the daughter.

———————

Salvo. Sirens sound.

———————

National anthem. They throw in handfuls of earth. The New
Leader walks away. His movements are quick.

———————

A thud. (Later people insisted that it was DROPPED and the
coffin webs weren't removed. According to folk wisdom that
means the deceased will be forgotten. I strongly disagree

with this. The thud coincided with the salute. There were only two grave-diggers and the coffin was heavy.

Relatives. Grave-diggers fill in the grave quickly. Grave is decked (?), with mourning crape.

Hat off. Puts it on.

Sirens sounding all over the country.

---

5 minutes' silence and all work stops.

They decorate the grave.

Parade of troops to the accompaniment of Chopin's "Funeral March". Does this symbolize continuation of the good work?

"Glory, glory, glory! . . ."
"Strength, strength, might! . . ."

The military wearing high boots – beautiful. But there are the airmen in ankle-length boots, and that's ugly.

———

Sailors, fine lads. Carrying carbines.

———

Border guards.

———

The conductor. Vigorously conducting the military orchestra. Waving his arms about energetically.

———

Again the journalist K.: "Rest assured, dear departed, that the banner of October is in reliable hands ..."

———

Again a black bird flies over Red Square. Close-up. Wonder what that means in folk superstitions. It's not the soul, is it?

———

The bird flew over, and that's all!

———

13:00

———

THAT'S ALL ...

... all, Ferfichkin, not a word now, there have been more than were necessary anyway. In exactly 9 hours and 15 minutes the New Year will arrive, and a new, bright life will begin, so – away with all sorrows, worries and disquiet! A new, indefatigable life will illuminate our steep banks, and part of our sorrow will vanish into the distant, or perhaps the recent, past, and worries and disquiet will at last leave us alone. That's nice! It's nice at home. At home there's a smell of baking. The pies are coming on nicely in the oven. My wife and I are seeing in the New Year on our own. I love pies, I love my wife, and I love my Homeland. I'm glad that the sorrow has passed, and that winter has come again, and that the December thaw has finally come to an end, as the lady on Channel One on Central Television has just announced. Happy New Year, friends, here's to new happiness, Ferfichkin ... Let's drink to the health and repose of all the persons appearing in all my epistles to you, let's drink to Garigozov, Kankrin, Sheponin, Galibutaev, Revebtsev, Kodzoev, Telelyasov, Popov, Gorich, Sholokhov, Razin, Natalya Evgenyevna, Uncle Kolya no. One and Uncle Kolya no.Two, Auntie Masha, Blanter, Mokrousov, Solovyov-Sedoi, Mother Tanya and Grandad Vanya, Sonya and Valya, the polar explorer Papanin, Yves Montand, Grandad Pasha, Mark Bernes, Kaledin, S.Anderson, my niece Manya, Taras Bulba and his sons, Karamzin, Mandelstam, Vertinsky, Grandad Sasha, Evgenya, Tsar Alexander the Second the Liberator, A.P.Chekhov and his father and brothers, to HIM WHO ONCE WAS, my cousin Sasha, Granny Marisha the First and Granny Marisha Stepanovna, the teacher Kanashenkov, P., now a well-known Soviet writer, Auntie Ira, my sister Natasha and niece Ksenya, Kuzmovna, Fyodor who makes musquash hats, Uncle Gosha and his son Pyotr,

Ninka-the-thief, honest Kotya, Uncle Vanya from Eniseisk, the Vlasovite Nikulchinsky, the drunkard Nikolai and his wife who was nicknamed "Demyan", the lodger Anna Konstantinovna, Dostoevsky, Leskov, Tolstoy, Mussorgsky, Chekhov, Kuprin, Gorky, Bunin, Merezhkovsky, the artist M., Grandad Evgeny and his children – Anatoly, Vsevolod, and Concordia, to the photographer Upatkin, the 69-year-old poet L., native of Odessa, and his splendid wife, L., also a poet, but of the female gender, and to his grammar school teacher, to my great uncle, who went off on horseback to Harbin, the editor who smelled of French perfume and Russian mists, the cook Dusya, Tatyana Gerasimovna from the journal, the Tsareviches Kan and Iliten, Ermak, Kuchum, Tsar Boris, the formalist Schwitters, my friend Romasha, the director F., my comrade Yu. from the city of Vienna, the major in the police and the major who spent all the war disseminating counter-propaganda in German, to comrade N. whose anniversary I celebrated, the bald-headed writer Plastronov (let's be kind, as it's Christmas), the Princes Trubetskoi and Gagarin, D.A.Prigov, A.Blok, Granny Felitsata Stepanovna, Nadson, Vasily Anisimovich, Anisim Sevastyanovich, all the Krasnopeevs, Koreisha the boss and Koreisha the God's fool, Shota Rustaveli, the clown Mamalyga, Pushkin, Nekrasov, Fet, to Anfyushka-the-nun and Grandad the beggar, to M.V.Lomonosov, V.I.Ulyanov, to Uncle Volya, Andryusha-the-store-keeper, the Korean Tsoi, the official folklore narrator Fyokla Chichaeva, Nefed Nefedych, the playwright Bruegel, M.Bulgakov, the men of the '60s U. and Yu., the fairy-story writer S., the outstanding writer Zh., my litbro E. and his wife and child, the black-marketeer Firs, D.Minaev, the actor Urbansky, Evgeny Anatolyevich, Lev Isaakovich, Felix Feodosyevich, the former philosopher K., to that lady, the child of the '60s, and that lady who is always denouncing people to me, to

178

Yu.V.Trifonov, Freud, Sterne, Babel, Zoshchenko, Nabokov, Kataev, Vivaldi, Mozart, Bach, to A., the great poet of contemporaneity (female gender), to K.Leontiev, to F.Kafka, B.Ryurikov, Andrei Bely, Gogol, Ogaryov, Herzen, Iskander, to Pantyushev, Filatov and Tryndin – the owners of the buildings on the Arbat that brought in the money, to M.G. – the Hero of Socialist Labour, to Ark. Gaidar, Evg. Kharitonov, Sergei P. and his ex-wife, Galya the cross-eyed beauty, to B.E.Trosh, my dear comrade, to Vasily Aksyonov, Okudzhava, Evtushenko, Voznesensky, to the Komsomol organizer S.Ivanov, to the official at VAAP, to the architects Iktin, Callicrates, D.I.Gilardi, L.A.Teplitsky, S.B.Zalessky, E.L.Yokhelis, S.Karin, P.S.Egerev, D.N. Chechulin, M.B.Posokhin, A.A.Midoyants, Kalugin, V.I. Dolganov, to the sculptors N.A.Andreyev, A.P.Kilbalnikov, P.K.Klodt, Phidias, to the directors Dunaev and Efros, to I.Kalman, G.Yaron, N.Belokhvostikova, A.Pugacheva, to Vladimir Spiridonovich Gigauri, Vadik Repin, P.G. Smidovich, N.S.Khrushchev, K.A.Timiryazev, V.Mayakovsky, Elena Kozlova, Huxley, Joyce, Dos Passos, Zamyatin, Remizov, Ehrenburg, Pantaleimon Romanov, Dobychin, Céline, Vitasik the Deaf and Sanya Morozov the First, the poet Andron Voskresensky and Zina Magranzh from the "Red Guard" publishing house, to the teacher B. and the whole of the Russian alphabet, to I.D.Sytin and P.B. Sytin, to the artist who was the creator of the poster that was so famous, and his son Garik, to the intellectual Rufa, to the theatre expert by calling and profession and literary critic Sh., to my friend from the Miniature Theatre, to Stanislavsky and Nemirovich-Danchenko, to Tairov, to the lessee Ya.V.Shchukin, to the geniuses E. and Sh., to Leonid Gubanov, the Tsvetaevas – A.I. and M.I., to A.Volodin, Grisha Strukov, to those fine lads who loaded up the empties at the shop and to all the women who work in the "Little Nip" bars in Moscow, to O.Tabakov, the artist Teodor and the man he shares the communal apartment with, to the little boy Fedya, whom I want to introduce to my niece Manya, to V.Vysotsky, Bruegel Senior, D.P.Tatishchev, the famous Soviet playwright P. (female gender), to the editor, comrade Ch., to the top officials, to the journalist K., to the New Leader, to A.Leshchev, E.Prusonov and many, many others, to you, to me, to my wife, to our common Homeland.

Shall we drink?

Moscow
31 December 1982

NOTES

NOTE ON TRANSLATION

It is not unusual for translators to make special pleas, but the grounds for doing so in the present instance seem to me particularly strong. Popov's style is highly idiomatic and eclectic in the extreme. His novel abounds in parodies of Soviet jargon, in current slang, archaisms and snatches of poetry. Some passages are "straight" and are to be taken at face value. At times the style can be unashamedly elevated – the novel's subtitle alone caused the translator a good deal of agonizing, and at last it was felt that "epistles", which appropriately retains the literary and biblical flavour of the original, was to be preferred to either "missives" or simply "letters". Acronyms and abbreviations occur frequently. There are many allusions which a Soviet reader will respond to immediately, but which are wasted on the foreigner. On a few occasions the pre-Revolutionary orthography is used. Add to all this the ubiquitous typographical idiosyncracies and the odd neologism and the problems of rendering the text adequately in English should be apparent.

To keep footnotes to a minimum I have spelled out in full all but the best-known abbreviations – the full form in English still retains, in my view, the ponderous, inelegant quality of the original. There are some minor adjustments to the text as published in the journal *Volga* (vol.ii 1989). These have been made at the request of the author, or with his consent, the better to make his point without further footnoting.

page 6   *The Don as in Sholokhov* . . .: The reference is to the epic novel *The Quiet Don* by Mikhail Sholokhov (1905–1984).

6   *Along the bank of the Don* . . .: these words are from a popular folk song.

6   *Stenka Razin* (d.1671): famous cossack rebel.

6 *Alexei Kaledin* (1861–1918): Don Cossack leader of White resistance to the Bolsheviks.

7 *I spend manee . . .*: these words appear in transliterated English in the original.

8 *Another currency reform*: There were in fact currency reforms in both 1947 and 1961 which adversely affected people's savings.

8 *"I've left you, my dear ones . . ."*: from *Letters of a Russian Traveller* by Karamzin (see below).

9 *Nikolai Karamzin* (1766–1826): historian, poet and journalist. His major work was *The History of the Russian State*, a more literary than scholarly undertaking.

9 *Taras Bulba*: Nikolai Gogol (1809–1852) based the eponymous hero of this work on a number of historical figures who led the Zaporozhye cossacks against the Poles from the fifteenth to the seventeenth centuries.

9 *Osip Mandelstam* (1891–1938): one of the greatest of Russia's poets, he was exiled to Voronezh for his criticism of Stalin. He was later re-arrested, and died in a camp near Vladivostok.

10 *Natalya Evgenyevna Shtempel* (1908–1988): a close friend of Osip and Nadezhda Mandelstam. Osip dedicated several poems to her.

10 *Vasily Tyorkin*: the eponymous "common soldier" hero of a popular World War II poem by Alexander Tvardovsky (1910–1971).

12 *Taganrog*: the birth place of Anton Chekhov (1860–1904), mentioned several times in the course of the novel.

16 *Fetisov*: a writer invented by Popov. He figures fleetingly in this novel on two or three occasions, as well as in several other stories.

18 *Kulak*: a rich peasant. The term was often one of abuse. In the 1930s, when the land was collectivized, Stalin liquidated the kulak class.

18 *Port Arthur*: scene of famous battle in the Russo-Japanese War (1904–1905).

18 *PUSSY CAT MYTH . . . Yves Montand*: there is a phonetic connection between the name of the French singer and the Russian word for "myth".

22 *Always room for the heroic deed* . . .: a well-worn quotation from *The Old Woman Izergil* by Maxim Gorky (1868–1936), often regarded as the father of Soviet literature.

23 *Lavrenty Beria* (1899–1953): head of Stalin's security service from 1938, until he was liquidated when Khrushchev came to power.

23 *1956* . . .: this was the year of the Twentieth Party Congress, at which Khrushchev denounced Stalin's policies. Consequently, many victims of the purges were rehabilitated – thousands of political prisoners and exiles were allowed to return to European Russia.

23 *Decembrist gentry*: liberal-minded revolutionary aristocrats, who in December 1825 attempted to overthrow Nicholas I. The leaders were hanged and many others sent into Siberian exile.

26 *Manifesto of 19 February*: the Edict of the Emancipation of the serfs was issued on 19 February 1861. Some of the preceding sentences relate to "The Toupée Artist", a story by Nikolai Leskov (1831–1895) about the iniquities of serfdom.

26 *Anton Chekhov* (1860–1904): this most cultivated and humane writer was one generation removed from peasant stock. His statement that he had to "squeeze the serf out of himself drop by drop" is often quoted.

27 *Tyoply Stan*: a not particularly fashionable, far-flung suburb of Moscow.

29 *Only the concrete pillars flashing by* . . .: a parody of lines from Pushkin's poem "The Demons".

30 *Vlasovite*: a Soviet coinage for the worst kind of traitor. General Andrei Vlasov (1900–1946) was captured by the Germans in 1942 and fought on their side.

31 *Shock-worker* . . . *Stakhanovite*: Alexei Stakhanov was a Donbass coalminer who vastly exceeded his work norm in one shift in 1935, thus initiating the "Stakhanovite" or "shock-worker" movement.

32 *A., a great poet of contemporaneity*: Bella Akhmadulina (born 1937).

35 *Ivan Fyodorov* . . . *metallic eyes*: Ivan Fyodorov (c.1510–1583) was the founder of printing in Russia. This passage

185

refers to his statue, situated quite near Dzerzhinsky Square, the site of the Lubyanka (KGB headquarters). Hence there are connotations of fear and silence.

36 *The poet L . . .*: Semyon Lipkin (born 1911).

36 *Pyotr Shchetinkin* (1885–1927): a prominent leader of Bolshevik partisan units in Siberia during the Civil War (1918–1921).

39 *Perfume and Russian mists . . .*: these words are reminiscent of lines in the poem "The Unknown Woman" by Alexander Blok (1880–1921)

41 *The battle, the last for Kuchum . . .*: the quotation is from the *History of the Russian State XVI–XVII centuries*. See note above on Karamzin.

42 *The escalating waste . . .*: the point of the quote from *Pravda* is to show the value of creative writing, as against sterile Soviet journalese.

42 *Mice-like scuttling of life . . .*: a near quotation from Pushkin's poem "Lines Composed at Night during Insomnia".

45 *No ordinary day . . .*: the October Revolution is celebrated on 7 November with a public holiday.

46 *The Time of Troubles*: the period of political turmoil from 1598 to 1613. The State of Muscovy virtually disintegrated at times during this period, and Poland, supporting various false pretenders to the throne, invaded the country.

46 *Trubetskois*: the Trubetskoi family was very prominent throughout modern Russian history. For example, Sergei Trubetskoi (1790–1860) was one of the leaders of the Decembrist plot. See note above.

47 *Church of Anna, where according to rumours . . .*: the rumours have been largely substantiated. The church apparently houses a vast quantity of art treasures and books, some from Hitler's private collection (see the *Independent on Sunday* 28 April 1991).

48 *Alexander Blok* (1880–1921): leading Symbolist poet and playwright. See above.

49 *Evgeny Kharitonov*: see Author's footnote on p.101

49 *"The Blue Light"*: a popular light entertainment programme on television in the 1960s. It was revived at the

end of the 1970s. Generally screened on public holidays, such as 7 November, it provided a most welcome contrast to the more turgid fare usually served up by the media at the time.

50   *When a cannon in old Petersburg ...*: a reference to the battleship *Aurora* firing a (blank) shell at the time of the Bolshevik coup.

51   *Nestor Makhno* (1889–1934): leader of the anarchist, anti-Bolshevik group in the Ukraine during the Civil War of 1918–1921.

51   *BAM*: the Baikal-Amur Railway, the second trans-Siberian railway. Though under construction since the 1950s, it was very much a symbol of the Brezhnev era. Work on it continues in a desultory manner to this day.

51   *I once popped out ...*: here one should recall the author's own experiences after the *Metropol* affair. See *Translator's Preface*.

54   *Semyon Nadson* (1862–1887): poet who displayed great awareness of social injustices.

54   *Yellowy in colour*: yellow sometimes has connotations of craziness in Russian.

56   *Fantomas*: a character in Gaston Leroux's stories, an amateur detective, noted for his bald, bullet-shaped head. The French films based on the stories are well known in Russia.

56   *Died of consumption in 1937 ...*: 1937 saw the height of Stalin's purges.

57   *Old foreign gob*: Stalin was Georgian. His appearance and accent have been much commented on, not least by his detractors.

58   *Layabouts of ... Aldan*: Aldan, in the Yakut ASSR, is well-known for its tramps and drop-outs. The area is rich in mineral deposits and Popov once worked there in his time as a geologist. The origin of the Russian word for "layabout" here is interesting: *bich* is both a corrution of the English "bitch" and the initials of a phrase meaning "A former intelligent (or intellectual) person". A *bich* might occasionally obtain seasonal work, and may well have had a spell in prison.

60   *The Dalton Plan*: developed in Dalton, Massachusetts, this
      scheme for education based on individual learning was
      fashionable in the Soviet Union and various parts of Europe
      in the 1920s.

62   *Mikhail Lomonosov* (1711–1765): outstanding writer and
      scholar, one of the founders of Moscow University.

67   *Author's sheets*: In Russia writers are paid by the page. An
      "author's sheet" is 40,000 typed characters for prose and
      700 lines for poetry.

67   *I study, I study* . . .: Lenin's much-quoted injunction was
      "Study, study, study".

68   *And burdock will grow* . . .: perhaps a parody of the end
      of the novel *Fathers and Sons* by Ivan Turgenev (1818–
      1883).

68   *Baron Karl Münchhausen* (1720–1797): soldier and
      notorious teller of tall stories.

68   *Oblomovism*: Oblomov was the eponymous slothful hero of
      the novel by Ivan Goncharov (1812–1891). He spends much
      of his time on his divan.

68   *In an old book* . . .: see Ecclesiastes III: 5.

71   *Halfway to the moon*: There is a story of this name by
      Vasily Aksyonov (born 1932) (See *Translator's Preface*),
      first published in 1962.

72   *"We're not playing for money."*: a quotation from
      Pushkin's fragment "Faust in Hell".

72   *Svidrigailov's America*: the degenerate Svidrigailov in
      Dostoevsky's *Crime and Punishment*, says that he plans to
      go to America, just prior, in fact, to committing suicide. He
      also recommends America to the hero Raskolnikov, as a
      country that might better acccommodate the hero's
      outlandish values.

73   *It's really, really new, like Popov's name to you*: Popov is,
      in fact, a very common, old Russian name, though the
      author is relatively new to the literary scene.

75   *E., My literary brother in misfortune*: Viktor Erofeev (born
      1947). See *Translator's Introduction*.

76   *Alla Pugacheva*: a popular contemporary singer.

76   *Just like Lev Tolstoy* . . .: the reference here is to Tolstoy's
      comment, in variously reported versions, on the writer

Leonid Andreev, that he "tries to scare people, but I'm not afraid".

76   *Konstantin Leontyev* (1831–1891) : conservative political thinker.

78   *A party member* ...: here, as elsewhere in the text, the word "party" does not appear in the original, thus providing an obscene *double entendre*.

79   *300 ether valerian drops* ...: the reference is to Koroviev in *The Master and Margarita* by Mikhail Bulgakov (1891–1940)

81   *Quoth the Raven* ...: the primary reference here is to Edgar Poe's poem "The Raven", but note also that in Pushkin's *The Mermaid* the old man refers to himself as a raven.

83   *NEW LEADER*: the choice of words here is highly significant. The Russian term used in the first published text is "rukovoditel", a word denoting a degree of banality, but essentially a neutral term which could be rendered as "man in charge". However, in the original draft the author uses "vozhd", a designation first adopted by Stalin, revived by Brezhnev in his later years, and not dissimilar in connotations to the German "führer". The author's preference now is for this term and it has been rendered accordingly.

84   *So humble yourself* ...: a parody of "Humble yourself, proud man", the words Dostoevsky addressed in his "Pushkin Speech" of 1880 to Pushkin's hero Evgeny Onegin.

84   *No day without a page* ...: Yury Olesha (1899–1960) wrote a book called *No Day without a Line* (published, incidentally, posthumously). The subsequent sentences – and later passages – should be read in the context of calls by Andropov, Brezhnev's immediate successor, for more discipline in the work place.

85   *I've just got on to the 35th now* ...: this page number coincides with the 35th page (numbered 37) of the novel as first published in the journal *Volga* no.ii. 1989.

85   *Have a complete rest* ...: the reference is to the closing words of Chekhov's play.

88 *Paramon the Martyr's day* . . .: these are all events in the
Russian Orthodox calendar, largely self-explanatory, with
the exception of the "First Voice" – there are eight voices,
taken over from the Greek Orthodox church, which signify
the singing of angels.

89 *Herzen and Ogaryov . . . Sparrow Hills* . . .: Alexander
Herzen (1812–1870), political radical thinker, and his friend
Nikolai Ogaryov (1813–1877) took a solemn oath on the
Sparrow Hills (currently the Lenin Hills), in Moscow, not to
forget the example set by the Decembrists. See note above
on Decembrists.

89 *My friend K* . . .: Vladimir Kormer (1939–1987). Though he
worked on the journal *Questions of Philosophy*, he was also
a novelist and short story writer, winning the 1978 Dahl
prize, awarded in Paris, for his novel published in
emigration *The Mole of History*. In 1990 another novel
Inheritance was published, this time in the Soviet journal
Oktyabr.

90 *LIBERTÉ . . . AEROPORT* . . .: the district of Moscow around the
Aeroport metro station is inhabited by many of the liberal-
minded intellectuals, who none the less are sometimes
inclined to conform. On coming to power Andropov was
sometimes seen in such quarters as something of a liberal,
though there was no evidence for this. K. is parodying,
good-naturedly, those intellectuals who pretend to know
more than they really do.

91 *Yury Trifonov* (1925–1981). His novel *The House on the
Embankment* deals with the problems of the purges and
careerism from the 1930s to the 1970s. The hero's father, an
exceedingly cautious man, always used to warn his children
to obey the signs on the trams and not "lean out".

95 *Valentin Kataev* (1897–1986): leading prose writer and
dramatist. He developed the artistic notion of "mauvisme"
in the 1960s whereby he defended experimentation and
innovation, arguing that, since everyone seemed to be
writing well, the best policy was to write badly.

96 *Forty Orthodox days* . . .: in Russia a service is held forty
days after a person's death.

96 *DEATH HAVING* ...: These words are taken from the Russian Easter service.

97 *Borodino, Smolensk, Berezina* ...: Scenes of famous battles during Napoleon's invasion of and retreat from Russia.

97 *Decembrism*: see note above on Decembrists.

97 *Senate Square*: during the Decembrist revolt the rebel troops and units loyal to the Tsar faced each other on Senate Square in front of St Petersburg's Winter Palace.

97 *Nerchinsk*: the place where the Decembrists did penal servitude.

98 *Take care of yourself, comrade* ...: one might recall here the 75-year-old Brezhnev standing for hours on the mausoleum for the October Revolution celebrations on the 7 November, with the Russian winter approaching.

98 *"With a sharp little eye"*: a quotation from *Solitaria* by Vasily Rozanov (1856–1919), religious thinker and writer. The sense here is that one Russian looks at another in a certain way and immediately they understand each other.

99 *"He ought to ring us up."*: i.e. the new leader, Yury Andropov.

99 *Music of explosion and breaking* ...: this is something of an inversion of Blok's famous statement about hearing the "music of the Revolution".

101 *"The Prague"*: The "Prague" restaurant is notoriously difficult to get into.

102 *"Scrape-scrape peg leg."*: this refers to a Russian fairy story in which a bear with a wooden leg comes back at night to eat the person who cut its leg off.

103 *"The Jolly Wits' Club"*: A popular satirical TV programme of the 1960s. The initials in Russian (KVN) also denote, incidentally, the trade name of the first, rather primitive, Soviet-produced television set.

103 *Okudzh ... Evtush ... Voznesensk ... Luzhn* ...: The unfinished proper nouns are Okudzhava, Evtushenko, Voznesensky and Luzhniki. Bulat Okudzhava is best known for his guitar-accompanied songs, Evgeny Evtushenko and Andrei Voznesensky for their poetry, though all three have

excelled in other genres too. Closely associated with the more liberal times of the '60s and the public performances at Luzhniki, they none the less retained official approval by adapting to the harsher climate under Brezhnev. The narrator is so weary of these names – oft repeated at home and abroad when other writers just as deserving received no recognition – that he cannot be bothered to finish them.

105 *"Ah, play 'ccordian, play."*: though Sergei P. is a Jew, he behaves exactly like a Russian here, singing a lively Russian song and drinking immoderately.

107 *"Cult of personality"*: a euphemism for Stalinism and the purges.

111 *Even in the forests and swamps* . . .: The graffiti here depend on a very clever, untranslatable pun: the words are a near quotation from Pushkin's *The Bronze Horseman*, involving the archaic word for "marshes", which appears in a form identical to the modern Soviet word for "the old-boy network", or obtaining goods and services through connections and influence.

112 *VAAP*: the All-Union Copyright Agency, established in 1973.

113 *Georg Ots* (1920–1975): Estonian baritone.

113 *Scientific-technical revolution* . . .: one of the shibboleths of the Brezhnev era.

114 *"Vremya"*: nightly TV news programme.

116 *Lublin* . . . *Lyublino* . . .: free association between the city in Eastern Poland and a town in Russia.

118 *Famous literary events* . . .: the *Metropol* affair (See *Translator's Preface*).

120 *"Billy Bones"*: the title refers to the character in Stevenson's *Treasure Island*. Popov's story has now been published (*Vest*, Knizhnaya palata, Moscow, 1989).

123 *Journey from Petersburg* . . .: the name of this game recalls *Journey from Petersburg to Moscow*, the exposé of social injustice under Catherine the Great by Alexander Radishchev (1749–1802). Given the Leningraders' vote in 1991 to revert to the original name for their city, the joke here is perhaps all the more poignant. The "game" in fact had no rules, and just involved a lot of vodka-drinking and anti-communist joke-telling.

126 *TimERZYAev*: the typography here is not just a parody of Kataev's theory of "mauvisme" (See above), but produces a pun – "merzavets" means "scoundrel".

126 *Togetherness*: the Russian term here, *sobornost*, is sometimes translated as "conciliarism". It denotes community spirit, particularly within the Russian church, and is a quality much favoured by the Slavophiles.

137 *"Agitator and rebel rouser"*: this was how Vladimir Mayakovsky (1893–1930) described himself in his poem "At the Top of My Voice".

137 *YSOG*: (Russian initials SMOG). This was a literary society of the 1960s, whose members included Leonid Gubanov, Sasha Sokolov and Yury Kublanovsky.

138 *Leonid Gubanov* (1946–1983): poet and member of YSOG (see above). Despite the author's disclaimer, the description of E. here does bear a remarkable resemblance . . .

138 *Marina Tsvetaeva* (1892–1941): with Ahkmatova, Mandelstam, and Pasternak, Tsvetaeva was one of the four great Russian poets of the twentieth century.

139 *Kataev*: See above.

141 *PETROVKA-38*: headquarters of the Moscow police, the equivalent of Scotland Yard.

141 *Must get on with the business . . .*: these words recall a passage in Chekhov's "A Boring Story" in which a professor rebukes a lazy student.

142 *Vladimir Vysotsky* (1938–1980): poet-guitarist and actor.

145 *One charming November evening . . .*: the tone here is heavily ironic, and refers to events following the appearance of the second almanach that Popov was involved in, *Katalog* (Ardis 1981). Popov and others were subjected to house-searches – at the time he was indeed living in the flat of the prototype for Nefed Nefedych. His manuscripts were confiscated, and when most, but not all, were returned, he was officially informed that he was under the surveillance of the KGB and the Public Prosecutor's Office for: (1) contact with the renegade V. Aksyonov, (2) creating ideologically harmful, near-pornographic and slanderous works, and (3) communicating slanderous information to Western correspondents.

148 *My life in art* ...: perhaps reminiscent of *My Life in Art* by Konstantin Stanislavsky (1863–1938).

150 *All my manuscripts were lost* ...: see note above.

152 *The iron horses* ...: i.e. on the Bolshoi Theatre building.

153 *P* ...: Lyudmila Petrushevskaya (b.1938).

156 *"Chopped up ... just like Oleg Tabakov*: the reference is to the play *In Search of Joy* by Viktor Rozov (born 1913), in which the 15 year-old Oleg Savin smashes up the furniture with a sabre. The role was one of the most famous to be played by the prominent actor and director Oleg Tabakov.

171 *"Dizziness from success"*: this was the cynical title of Stalin's notorious article which signalled a slackening of the pace in his collectivization policy, a policy which had had catastrophic results on Soviet agriculture.

157 *"Weightily, tangibly ..."*: these words are reminiscent of lines in Mayakovsky's "At the Top of My Voice" (see above).

163 *Sparrow Hills*: see note above on Herzen and Ogaryov. One should also perhaps bear in mind the finale to Bulgakov's *The Master and Margarita*, when the devil and his retinue quit Moscow.

168 *We're off!*: the narrator has in mind the words used by Yury Gagarin, the first man in space, on take-off.